THE LIQUIDATOR

Hand-picked for his talents by Mostyn, the suave, sadistic Second-in-Command of British Special Security, Boysie Oakes's job is to quietly murder potential Top Security risks – but is Boysie the right man for the job? Things begin to go wrong for Boysie when he takes Mostyn's secretary to the Côte D'Azur for a naughty weekend. What starts as a few days of seduction in the Mediterranean sun turns into a nightmare for Boysie as he becomes more and more embroiled in Operation Coronet.

THE LIQUIDATOR

THE LIQUIDATOR

by

John Gardner

Magna Large Print Books
Long Preston, North Yorkshire,
BD23 4ND, England.

British Library Cataloguing in Publication Data.

Gardner, John
    The liquidator.

    A catalogue record of this book is
    available from the British Library

    ISBN   0-7505-2353-0

First published in Great Britain in 1964 by
Frederick Muller Ltd.

Copyright © 1964 by John Gardner

Cover illustration © John Hancock by arrangement with
P.W.A. International Ltd.

The moral right of the author has been asserted

Published in Large Print 2005 by arrangement with
John Gardner, care of Coombs Moylett Literary Agency

Magna Large Print is an imprint of Library Magna Books Ltd.

Printed and bound in Great Britain by
T.J. (International) Ltd., Cornwall, PL28 8RW

For Jane, Robert and Thelma

My grateful thanks to Captain E Mercer DFC for technical assistance with regard to jet aircraft. Captain Mercer should not, however, be held responsible for any pilot error made by the author in Chapter Nine. JG

CONTENTS

PROLOGUE: PARIS

August 1944

Mostyn was fighting for his life. Twice he had thrown the short one into the gutter, but now they were both at him: the short one trying to pinion his arms while the big fellow's hands were almost at his throat. He was tiring now, sweating and furious: furious with himself for being caught like this. It was an object lesson in lowering one's guard while still operational.

That morning he had seen British tanks in the Place de la Concorde. He had whistled all the way back to Jacques' flat – feeling that life was his again. The job was nearly over – and now, to be jumped by the very two men he had so carefully avoided during the past long six weeks. It was unforgivable.

The big one reached for his throat: he could feel himself being pressed against the wall: the cold bricks hard at the back of his neck as he pushed his chin down on to his chest to stop the great hot hands forcing through to his windpipe.

But the big man was winning: the world was going red. He could hardly breathe, and

13

the pain had begun to paralyse his shoulders and arms as he threshed about, panicking to set himself free. What a way to die – in a back alley off the Boulevard Magenta, with all Paris singing at her emancipation on this gorgeous afternoon.

Somewhere, far away beyond the waterfall noise in his ears, he thought he could hear the tanks again. One last effort. He heaved upwards with his arms, kicked out and brought his knee sharply between the big one's legs. He felt the knee-cap make a squashy contact. The man yelped and dropped back, growling a German oath before springing in again. Out of the corner of his eye, Mostyn saw something flicker farther up the street. Still grappling with the two men, he gave a quick turn of the head. The newcomer was running out of the sunlight at the alley entrance, the mottled camouflage jacket unmistakable. Mostyn shouted – shocked at the frightened falsetto of his own voice: 'Help! Quickly! I'm British! Help! Intelligence!'

The big fellow looked round, startled and off-guard. There was a moment's hesitation, then he began to stumble away. The little man had lost his balance, pushing himself from the wall in an attempt to follow his companion.

They only managed three steps – four at the most. To Mostyn, panting against the wall, the shots sounded like cannon fire. Then, suddenly, it was all over. The two Germans lay like crumpled piles of clothes – the big one sprawled face-down, his head resting on the pavement, a matted patch of spreading red where the base of his skull had been: the little one was on his back, a bullet through the neck, his eyes looking up with the reproachful surprise of one who has met his Maker unready and with unexpected swiftness.

Mostyn looked at his saviour. He was a sergeant: from a tank crew, judging by the accoutrements – map-case and binoculars – slung round his neck. Now the big Colt automatic seemed too heavy for him. His wrist sagged as though the weight was dragging it down; a thin trickle of blue smoke turning to wispy grey as it filtered from the muzzle, up the barrel and over his hand.

But it was the eyes that made Mostyn catch his breath, sending the short hairs tingling on the nape of his neck: ice-blue, cold as freezing point, looking down at the bodies with immense satisfaction.

Mostyn prided himself that he could read the truth in other men's eyes. These told the story all too plainly. This man, a perfect technician in death, had enjoyed shooting to kill. He was, thought Mostyn, a born assassin, a professional who would blow a man's life from him as easily, and with as little emotion, as he would blow his own nose.

The sergeant was still gazing at the corpses, his mouth curved slightly at one corner in a wry smile. This one, thought Mostyn, will be worth watching. One day he might be useful again.

1 – *LONDON*

Saturday June 8th 1963

BOYSIE

Boysie Oakes slid the razor smoothly over the last froth of lather below his chin and ran the side of his third finger carefully in its wake. Satisfied, he rinsed the razor, doused a flannel and proceeded to sponge away the surplus foam. Drying his face, a moment later, he paused, peering into the mirror, searching for the least sign of wear or tear.

For a man in his mid-forties, Boysie was in peak condition. Not a single fold of skin showed on the neck or up the hard jaw line. His mouth, with the built-in slight upward curve at the left corner, had not deteriorated into the full sensual thickness which he had once feared. Momentarily he turned his head, slanting his eyes to get a better look at the left profile which a woman had once called his 'Mona Lisa side'. The striking ice-blue eyes were as clear as they had been in his teens – the tiny laughter lines and minute crows' feet revealing a dependable maturity instead of the prophetic marks of encroaching age. Time had neither thinned his eyebrows nor pushed back his hairline: the only concession to approaching middle-age seemed to be the shining flecks of grey at his temples.

Boysie spilled a tiny pool of Lentheric *Onyx* into the hollow of his left palm, crossing it to the right and working the mixture up his long fingers before running both hands quickly down and over his cheeks and chin. His eyes twitched fractionally as the lotion stung into the pores, the clean tang catching at his nostrils. He followed it with a tiny puff of talc from the black and gold container, rubbing it down and away until no trace was visible.

Replacing the requisites of good grooming in the clear glass cupboard, he stepped away from the magnifying mirror, running the backs of his right-hand fingers to and fro over the freshly barbered jowl, now smooth as nylon stretched tight over arched female buttocks. His complexion – burnished by the daily half-hour stint with the sunray lamp – was as clear and tough as well-waxed leather, with none of the danger marks of purple-red veining under the eyes or at nose tip.

Ablutions completed, Boysie padded from the bathroom, across the carpeted passage into the luxurious little bedroom. Brubeck and his boys brought their arithmetically steady improvisation on Leonard Bernstein's *Somewhere* to its nostalgic climax. The record-player clicked as the next disc fell into position on the turntable and the liquid peace of Bach's *Goldberg Variations* filled the flat. The quiet pace of the harpsichord made Boysie feel more than usually conscious of the luck that had come his way.

Ten years ago he had never heard of the *Goldberg Variations,* or, for that matter, Matisse – one of whose original geometrically brilliant oils hung over the white and silver headboard of the big double bed. Boysie lit a king-sized filter and took a quick look at himself in the wall-length mirror. The picture seemed pretty good to him: his body, utterly male, hard, balanced and straight as a lath. He posed conceitedly – a Sunday heavy ad in azure string vest and Y-front briefs.

Coming out of the little fantasy, he took a long draw at his cigarette, rested it on the ashtray – which stood next to a deluxe copy of the *Kama Sutra* on the bedside table – and slipped a cream poplin tailored shirt over his head. Pulling out the tie rack, he selected a Thailand silk in bronze to match the autumn-tinted Courtelle suit which lay ready on the bed. Johann Sebastian's intricate keyboard practice weaved on.

Whatever else one felt about Mostyn, thought Boysie adjusting the waistband of his trousers, at least he was a *thorough* swine.

He was really deeply indebted to Mostyn. A complete new world had been opened up to him almost from the moment he had signed the Official Secrets Act, together with that ominous piece of paper which made him a particular slave to the Department of Special Security. Art, Literature, Music, the Drama, food, wine, the knowledge of a gourmet (if not the true palate) – all had been brought to him through Mostyn: together, of course, with the £4,000 a year, the regular bonuses and the white custom-built E-type Jaguar.

Fully dressed, he slipped his wrist-watch over the fingers of his left hand and glanced at the dial. Ten-thirty: must get going. For the second time that morning Boysie felt the disconcerting butterfly flutter in the pit of his stomach – always the prelude to flying. He walked into the living-room where the battered multi-labelled tan Revelation stood packed and locked; poured himself a double jigger of Courvoisier and pressed the stud that opened the secret drawer in his rebuilt Sheraton bureau. The small, pearl-handled automatic pistol lay snugly in its crimson velvet recess. He checked the mechanism and slid the weapon into the leather holster sewn into the hip pocket of his trousers, slipping the patent quick-release strap over the butt to keep it in place, and dropping three fully loaded spare magazines into the tailored clip on the inside pocket of his jacket. Mostyn would have a fit, he thought, if he knew of that gun. The business of only allowing him to go armed when on an actual assignment was one of the few things Boysie hated about the Department. There was no doubt that Mostyn would shoot up the wall with the agility of a monkey on a stick if he even heard of the existence of the weapon. But then, what Mostyn – now Second-in-Command of Security – believed about Boysie, and what Boysie *knew* about himself were as far removed from each other as the proverbial chalk and Stilton. When one really got down to cases, carrying that pistol – which couldn't be classed as a real man-stopper anyway – was Boysie's own private little joke against Mostyn. Even so, he invariably experienced a trickle of cold sweat whenever he thought too deeply on the consequences of Mostyn discovering his tiny secret.

The telephone jangled in the bureau recess. That would be Iris. He picked up the hand-piece and heard her voice – an amalgam of honey and rough sand – soft in his ear:

'Boysie?'

'Yes, sweetie?'

He could feel his body rise even at the sound of her. It had been like that for six months now – half a year of concentrated technique between assignments. She knew the game all right. When you dealt with the luscious Iris, it wasn't just a matter of one night in the Savoy Grill then oops into bed with no remorse. There had been moments of frustration of course, but, on the whole, Boysie had enjoyed the protracted love-play which, all being well, would end that very night on a bed not a spit from the palm fronds and surf of the Mediterranean. Again the spectre of Mostyn slunk quietly through his mind. One didn't take Mostyn's personal secretary for a dirty weekend on the French Riviera every day – and get away with it. Oh well, let's hope she's worth it, he thought.

'Boysie? I'm just leaving the flat. Everything all right?'

'Right as rain, sweetie. Don't worry about a thing. I'm going to ring the duty officer in a minute.' For a second he wondered if he was allowing his manner to assume too much urgency.

'You do think it'll be all right?'

'I've told you. Don't worry. Your boss never appears before midday on a Saturday, and by that time, sweetie, we'll be off into the wide blue yonder.' His stomach gave another twitch. There was silence, and for a moment he thought they had been cut off:

'Sweetie?'

'Yes, Boysie?'

'Don't forget, will you? You mustn't even notice me on the plane. Get a seat right up front, I'll sit at the back. We meet accidentally by the taxi rank outside Nice airport.

Got it?'

'Uh hu.'

'You go straight through the Customs' Hall and out of the swing doors; it's...'

'I know, Boysie...' she cut in on him, 'I've been there before...'

'And where else have you been, sweetie?'

'You'd be surprised.'

'I bet. Looking forward to it?'

'Of course.'

'You sound like a bride, darling.'

'See you, Boysie.' She had hung up on him. Still playing it distant, he smiled, dialling the Whitehall number. The signal burped at the other end and he heard a woman's crisp efficient voice.

'Mandrake Club.'– The code name for the day.

'I have a reservation. Number Two, please.' Better be on the safe side just in case Mostyn had come in early for a change.

'Do you want Number Two personally?'

'Yes.'

'He's not in yet.'

'OK. Give me Two Five.'

'Very good. One minute.' He heard the exchange click and a man's voice came on:

'Two Five. Duty Waiter.'

'This is "L",' said Boysie.

'Yes. Go ahead "L".'

'I'm off duty and want to catch some real sun...'

'One moment.' There was a pause. 'All right: yes, you're off duty, I was just checking.'

'I only wanted to say that I will be out of the country until Tuesday morning. In emergency you can get me at the Hotel Miramont, Menton, Alpes Maritimes, under my own name.'

'Understood. Thank you, "L". Behave yourself.'

'And you.' Mentally, Boysie gave him a 'soldier's farewell'.

He put down the receiver and grinned. In a grey building off Whitehall a young man sitting shirt-sleeved at a battery of coloured telephones made a note on an official file. 'Ten thirty-eight. Direct call from "L". "L" will be out of the country from a.m. today until a.m. Tuesday. Address, Hotel Miramont, Menton, Alpes Maritimes, France. Non-operational: under own name. Memos to Colonel Mostyn and pass to relieving D.O.' He pushed the slip across the desk to the honey-blonde secretary sitting at a small typing table in front of him. She smiled winningly and slid a sheet of paper into her typewriter. The Duty Officer of Special Security gazed into space and returned to pondering on the possibility of persuading the honey-blonde to spend Sunday at his flat in Knightsbridge – a vain hope, as he well knew that it was against the rules to frat with the hired help.

There was no doubt about it, Boysie was petrified with fear. It was the one thing that really worried and haunted him. Flying. Try as he could, the fear always swept into his guts just before take-off. The couple of twinges he had felt back in the flat were merely forerunners to the screaming terror that was now beginning to give him what Mostyn called 'the rectal twitch'. Seat belt tight across his midriff, he closed his eyes, and in a moment the whole wretched picture was clear. The Comet quivering on the runway. Brakes off. Wheels slashing the tarmac. The steep angle of climb; then, at about three hundred feet, the sudden, horrible shudder of engine failure or an incomprehensible error up on the flight deck.

There would be silence as the whole machine strained upwards against the sky, then dipped like some fairground monster to go whistling down. He could even hear the screams of his companions as he watched, from behind tightly shut lids, the slow-motion ball of fire and twisted metal gyrating towards him. Prophetically, the headlines of the evening papers were printed across his mind (HORROR AT LONDON AIRPORT), together with the familiar photograph of wreckage – a denuded tailplane pointing to the clouds, the ground mist of sinking smoke playing round a fireman's boots and, way down in column seven, his name among the bold-typed list of dead.

As the aircraft neared the turning point at the end of the runway, an arm of sunlight reached through the port nearest to him and, for a moment, the trick of light reflected his left eyebrow in the corresponding lens of his dark glasses. For a couple of seconds he glimpsed a bushy little forest speckled with tiny bulbs of sweat. He ran his hand over his forehead and blinked, feeling the pearls of water under his armpit change into rivulets, at the sudden movement, and trickle down his left side until they were blotted where his vest caught tight against the skin. His hands were unnaturally hot and his stomach jerked.

He dared not look around. A cursory glance as they had taxied away from the departure building had been enough. To the eye, his fellow travellers were unmoved by the imminent leap into the unusual environment of air and clouds. They looked calm, even matter-of-fact, chatty and relaxed. This was what he found so humiliating – the normal sense of loneliness magnified by the thought that he was the only terrified person among these insensible fleshlings: what rankled most was that, for him, it was so out of character.

Departure Building! Wasn't it the lounge at

Tokyo Airport which bore the sinister legend FINAL DEPARTURE? The fear, he told himself, was irrational. Must think of something else. Statistics showed that the chances of being killed in a commercial airliner were infinitesimal: smaller even than the chance you took crossing Piccadilly Circus. (Immediately Boysie remembered the morning when a taxi's mudguard had caught him a glancing blow on the right buttock just after he had stepped off the pavement opposite the Trocadero. 'Mind your arse, guv'nor!' The driver had shouted through a grin embellished with National Health dentures.)

Every time he flew, Boysie went through the same kind of personal hell; and after every trip, he swore that he would never do it again. But, in his kind of business, time and clients would not wait. The last occasion – only a week ago – had been a quick flight from London to Manchester, and he had been faced with the awful experience of sitting next to a man who, green-gilled, had muttered: 'The last time I was in an aeroplane, I was the only survivor.'

He wondered if Iris knew. Thank heaven she was not sitting with him, or behind him, to sense the fear. What would she think if she knew Boysie Oakes – Liquidator for Special Security – was transformed into a jelly at the thought of flying?

If he looked down the cabin he could see

her hand resting on the aisle seat five rows to his right; her forefinger running rhythmically up and down the edge of the ashtray, as though she were trying to smooth out the metal. Perhaps this was the outward sign of some inward trepidation. Perhaps she was frightened as well. But he would never know. Boysie could never bring himself to ask her – even if they ever did get to Nice!

'Good-morning, ladies and gentlemen. Captain Andrews and his crew welcome you on board this Comet of British European Airways. In a few minutes we will be taking off for Nice. We will be flying at a height of...' The stewardess' voice pattered out the mechanical greetings in English and French. Boysie blanched at the usual request for passengers to read the safety instructions, and the qualifying sentence about this being only a 'routine measure'.

Up on the flight deck, they were completing the long pre-take-off drill as the aircraft neared the threshold– '...rudder limiter out, cabin signs on, inverters on, fuel cocks check, radio check...' Cleared by Control, the big silver dart swept in a tight turn on to the runway, the Captain twisting the nose-wheel steering to line up for the final race into the air.

'All right, let's try this one.' Captain Andrews looked round. 'Give me full power.' The Flight Engineer leaned forward between the pilots' seats and put the flat of his hand across the throttles, holding them steady as the Captain eased the jets into their upwards roar.

'Full power.'

'Rolling.'

The rpm indicators showed a steady 8,000 as they trundled out; speed building up; the nosewheel hugging the centre of the tarmac; the horizon steady; the needles on the air-speed indicators travelling in their smooth arcs and the First Officer shouting above the noise:

'Airspeed both sides ... one hundred knots... V-One... Rotate!'

Andrews eased back on the control column yoke. The nose lifted and the ground fell away.

'V-Two ... noise abatement climb.' The Captain put the Comet into a steep full-power climb that took them up to one thousand five hundred feet in a matter of seconds, quickly reducing the earsplitting whine that fractured the nerves of householders in the immediate vicinity of the airport.

Boysie, still sitting rigid, retched, made a grab for the little brown bag poking from the net holder on the seat in front, and was noisily sick. The man sitting next to him looked embarrassed and turned away.

Later, after the illuminated sign – fasten seat belts. No smoking – had flicked off, the stewardess collected the bag, exchanging it for a large Courvoisier to settle the 'queasy tummy'.

'Something I ate last night,' lied Boysie. 'Been feeling a bit off ever since I got up.'

His neighbour swapped a knowing look with the stewardess, and Boysie pushed the cylindrical button under the chair arm, slid the seat back into the dental reclining position, closed his eyes and tried to blot the vacuum hum of engines from his mind.

As always at times of tension or stress, Boysie's lips began to move – showering a soundless stream of obscenities in the direction of Mostyn, the man he ever held responsible for any terror that came his way.

Slowly, as though the inaudible invective acted as a soporific, he seemed to relax. At the end of it all there would be Iris – lovely, lithe, athletic, red-haired Iris.

He lit a cigarette with the Windmaster, which bore his unfortunate monogrammed initials B.O, and contemplated the svelte behind of the stewardess as she bent over a passenger farther up the aisle. If Boysie had realised what confusion was about to be released by his lecherous and carefully planned Riviera jaunt, he would have been on his knees pleading to be taken home.

In a pink and white villa nestling on a terrace above the point where the Corniche In-

ferieure bends into Beaulieu-sur-Mer –
between Nice and Monaco – a man called
Sheriek was replacing the telephone receiver.

'The London people are really excellent,
my dear,' he said to the girl who was
engrossed in varnishing the toe-nails of her
right foot. 'He is on his way. Unfortunately,
there is a woman in tow, but I don't think
she will cause us much trouble – a minor
detail.'

The girl cursed mildly as a drop of Dior
135 spilled on to the hem of her eau de nil
housecoat.

Sheriek continued, his soft accent almost
running the words together: 'They also tell
me that our co-ordinator for this operation
– someone rather important – is en route. It
is up to us: we must show some enthusiasm,
my dear. In fact, I think we should take
steps before we are contacted, just to prove
that we are on the ball – as our American
friends so quaintly put it. A drink?'

At London Airport a young man in a
cavalry-twill suit was dialling a Whitehall
number and asking for 'Number Two.'

The Comet crossed the Channel coast,
nosing along the airways towards Nice.

2 – *LONDON*

Saturday June 8th 1963

MOSTYN

About five minutes after the Comet whistled out of the London area, James George Mostyn declaimed loudly, and with some venom, that Boysie Oakes was a bastard. Finding himself not wholly satisfied with this sentiment, he went on to add that Iris MacIntosh was a whore.

The telephone was ringing when Mostyn opened his office door, and he bellowed for Iris only a fraction of a second before recalling that this was her free weekend. The bell sounded ominously insistent, so, without going through his normal, precise routine by the hatstand, Mostyn crossed to the desk, swung himself into a sitting position on its corner, picked up the receiver and pushed his bowler on to the back of his head with the handle of his black-sheathed umbrella.

'Mostyn!' he barked in a manner suggesting that the caller could not have chosen a worse time to ring.

'Fly,' grunted a voice at the other end.

'What?' Mostyn sounded incredulous, the meaning of the odd salutation not clicking into place until after he spoke. There were over two hundred such monosyllabic references which, as 2IC of the Department of Special Security, he was supposed to carry around in his head – no mean feat when one considered the constantly changing pattern of individual code titles. This one, however, was comparatively easy, despite the fact that, on this particular morning, Mostyn was undoubtedly a mite hung-over. The Embassy party of the previous evening had later turned into a gymnastic and not unpleasant orgy for two – the ex-wife of an unseated Conservative MP playing a considerable, and somewhat exhausting part.

'Fly.' The voice repeated the official designation for the Department's duty stake-out man at London Airport.

'Fly,' retaliated Mostyn at a quizzical drawl. 'Well hullo, buttons.'

Martin, the airport man, looked out of the telephone booth into the long limbo of the main concourse in Queen's Building and sighed. Mostyn's little jokes were legend, and he had heard this one over two years ago while still at the Training Establishment.

Mostyn settled himself more comfortably on the desk corner – a short compact man of fifty-one, with the shrewd brown eyes of a water rat. He began to swing the umbrella backwards and forwards, controlling it with the thumb and forefinger so that it just missed the chiselled toe-caps of his black town brogues.

'And what can we do for you, old Fly?' The voice, as ever, was edged with boredom. Martin instinctively wondered whether his report was really worthwhile:

'Well, it's probably nothing to worry about, but I thought you ought to know...'

'You can never be too conscientious, Fly.'

'...one of your brighter boys has just left the country.'

'And who might that be?' Mostyn knew of three agents who were due out over the weekend and his immediate reaction was that Central Control had omitted to brief Fly. Someone would have to be peed upon from several thousand feet.

'It's "L".'

It was as though some hidden mechanism had sprung a loaded hypodermic needle hard into Mostyn's rump. The whole of his body stiffened; the condescending smile disappeared; the jaw sagged, and then the shoulders drooped. When he spoke, his voice had lost the soothing quality replacing it with a coat of black frost:

'Who?'

'"L".'

'When?'

'Now, just this moment.'

'Where?'

'Nice, by BEA Comet. I think...'

'One minute.'

The hat and umbrella were on the floor and Mostyn was at the other side of the desk before Martin had time to finish. He had whipped the key-chain from his pocket and was about to unlock his 'Most Personal' drawer when he caught sight of the Duty Officer's memo on top of the small stack of papers which lay square in the centre of the leather-edged blotter. His eyes quickly took in the message and there were signs of some relief. '...out of the country ... until a.m. Tuesday ... Miramont Hotel ... non-operational.' Of course. He remembered Boysie was on stand down.

'It's OK, Fly.' His voice was back to normal. 'He's on leave.'

All the same, it had given him a jolt. Mostyn was always apprehensive when Boysie did anything unexpected. Even now a warning bell pinged away in the sixth sense area of his mind. He hadn't had time to make a complete assessment of the situation, but there was something not quite right about Boysie going off like this. Damn it, the fellow had been in the office only yesterday afternoon. He hadn't mentioned it then. Why the sudden flight?

'There is one other small thing.'

'Yes?' Mostyn was cautious.

'Well, I don't suppose this is anything either, but I recognised one of the other passengers...'

'Yes.' Even more dubious.

'Er ... your secretary, Iris ... er ... Whatsername...'

'MacIntosh!... Iris MacIntosh!' His voice rose as his normally ruddy colour changed into a volcanic shade of crimson:

'Iris on the same flight as "L"?'

'Yes, but they weren't together...'

'Ha!' ejaculated Mostyn in utter derision.

'...In fact I saw them pass in the concourse. They just ignored one another.'

'That proves it then.'

'Looked as though they had never seen each other before.'

Mostyn said a very rude word.

It was immediately after replacing the receiver that Mostyn made the loud comments on Boysie's parentage and Iris's morals. In fact, he brayed so loudly that the plump girl with the big, badly brassiered breasts (whom the 2IC always seemed to get from the secretaries' pool when Iris was away) poked her head round the door:

'You called, Colonel Mostyn?'

'No, I did not bloody call,' he shrieked, 'but now that you're here you'd better go down to Personnel and get me Iris Mac-

Intosh's security file. Here.' He signed the request chit and threw it at her.

The piece of paper floated across the room, the lumpy girl making a sort of scooping dive at it. Her breasts performed a weird series of parabolas against the rust and white spotted blouse. Ought to have 'em air-conditioned, thought Mostyn. Why do fat girls always wear clothes decorated with spots?

After the secretary had bounced from the room, he sat down, rested his head on his hands, and concentrated on the situation. What the devil had got into them? They both knew the regulations. This wasn't just a matter of Boysie being a bit playful. The ruling was quite plain.

Civilian staff employed by The Department under the Grade 1 Schedule are forbidden (under Section B. Para. 1 of Special Security Standing Orders) to knowingly communicate, consort, attend public or private functions, or in any way meet or assemble with active serving members of The Department, other than on authorised duty and on premises known to, and prescribed by, their immediate supervising officers. Violation of this regulation is synonymous with a breach in the Official Secrets Act (See Sec.A, Para. 4, S.S.S.O.), and punishable by dismissal and up to 10 years' imprisonment for civilian employees: Court Martial in camera for serving members of The Department.

In other words, as Mostyn often observed to new members, 'Spies ain't allowed to meet the office birds after hours. Not on no account.'

It was logical enough. Agents in or out of the field, only needed the information most likely to affect them personally. Some knew perhaps only five or six of their colleagues – out of the hundreds who worked for the organisation. On the other hand, many of the civilian personnel had a much broader – one might even say, panoramic – view of the strength, deployment, conditions and overall work of the Department. The no fraternisation rule was there to protect both morale and the internal security of the whole complex network.

But how, in the name of Mata Hari, had this thing started? Boysie wasn't one to hang around the office. Mostyn swore again as memory landed the ball right on his own doorstep. Of course: the night of the big panic – about six months ago. There were no couriers and he had sent her, with the coded, sealed order, round to the flat off Chesham Place. Damn!

He picked up the telephone.

'I want a continental line. Get me...' he

paused, looking down at the memo, '…Get me the Hotel Miramont in Menton on the Côte D'Azure. Reception.' Then, as an afterthought: 'Tell them it's a … a Mr Bellchambers making some enquiries.'

With eyes fixed on the telephone, Mostyn proceeded to indulge in a reverie involving Boysie and several primitive instruments of torture. There was a particularly revolting variation of the water torture which, he recalled, the German SS had used – via the Spanish Inquisition. The subject was strapped down under a tap – he could see himself supervising the operation on Boysie – and a damp cloth placed on the tongue. A tiny stream of water was allowed to fall on the cloth. By the natural actions of swallowing and breathing, so induced, the cloth was drawn down into the throat – producing, so they said, an agonising feeling of suffocation. Mostyn had Boysie begging for mercy when the phone rang:

'Yes?'

'Your call to Menton.'

'Thank you. 'Allo, 'allo.'

'Hotel Miramont. Reception. Bonjour.'

'I am trying to trace a young lady called MacIntosh – a young English lady,' said Mostyn in accomplished French.

'Certainly. One moment, monsieur.' The woman far away in the cool foyer sounded discreet, all-understanding. There was a

40

pause: 'I am sorry, monsieur, we have no one registered in that name.'

'Oh dear, this is worrying. Are you perhaps expecting anybody, mademoiselle? Anybody English?' Another pause.

'Only an English couple later today, monsieur; but the name is not Maceentosh, it is, how do you say it? Ooks?'

'Ooks?'

'O-A-K-E-S. Ooks. Monsieur and Madame Ooks.'

'No, mademoiselle,' said Mostyn with definite pleasure. 'No. Monsieur and Madame Ooks I do not know. Thank you, mademoiselle.'

'You're welcome, monsieur. I am sorry we have not been of more service.'

'Au revoir, mademoiselle.'

'Au revoir, monsieur.'

That settled it. By the pen of his aunt, he'd fix the hash of Monsieur and Madame Ooks when they got back to London on Tuesday. He might even have a special deputation waiting at the airport to meet them. Boysie and Iris were flagrantly breaking the one internal regulation that the Chief held sacred. Indeed, even if this was only a mild carnal prank with no harm done, he was going to be hard put to keep it quiet. For, while Mostyn was ready to raise all Hades against Boysie and Iris, he was not prepared to see either of them leave

41

the Department altogether.

He looked down and saw that his hands were shaking:

'Oh Christ,' he blasphemed silently: for Boysie was Mostyn's special anxiety; his own private jumbo-sized cross; the thorn deep in his side; the one person who could turn the smooth, sure, cynical, sadistic Mostyn into a hairless jibbering nit-wit. When Boysie became involved in anything which even smacked mildly of nefarious dealing, Mostyn suffered the excruciating agonies of the damned. He lost whole nights of sleep and went cold from tip to toe at the very thought of Boysie getting mixed up in anything outside the Department. There were moments when he almost wished that his life had not been saved by the tall tank sergeant on that hot afternoon off the Boulevard Magenta. He reasoned also that some of his present anxiety was probably for Iris – she knew a lot but she couldn't possibly know what Boysie really was: and you could never tell with people like Boysie.

Yet sometimes he found it hard to believe that this lean, handsome man exulted in the power of immolation. Often, when Boysie turned up in the office after a job – grinning and cheerful – it was difficult to equate him with the very efficient, coolly professional hired killer. But that was certainly what he was. The Second-in-Command had seen it

42

for himself and noted the pathological truth deep in those cold blue eyes on the afternoon when Boysie had so neatly dispatched the two Nazi undercover men. That was why he had run a special check on the man – Sergeant Brian Ian Oakes – after he had returned to England following the Paris incident. And that was how it had begun. Strange, though, that between 1944 and 1956, he had not even clapped eyes on Sergeant Oakes. By the time Boysie turned up again, so much had occurred that he had almost erased the Paris business from his mind.

Mostyn leaned back in his swivel chair, placed the tips of his fingers together in an attitude of prayer and thought about those few decisive days which had led to the recruitment of 'L' – Brian Ian ('Boysie') Oakes.

Boysie's advent into the Department had been sudden and dramatic. In the spring of '56 Mostyn was appointed Second-in-Command. Almost immediately he found himself scuttling off to Berlin to sort out a delicate matter involving a double-agent who had threatened to sell information to the CIA. He returned to find that, in his absence, chaos had come again.

In the space of one week there had been two enormous leaks from the Aircraft

Research Establishment. Two days later, without any consultation with the Department, Scotland Yard's Special Branch – normally the executive arm of both MI5 and Special Security – had arrested a Royal Air Force officer and a civilian typist on charges involving the Official Secrets Act. Several cabinet ministers, a swarm of MPs and most of the national Press were now bleating about the inefficiency of security. They were after somebody's blood – notably the top brass of the Department.

It was early on a Saturday morning when Mostyn flew back into London to find a trail of urgent messages, each couched in strong language, and all demanding his immediate presence before the Chief.

'I'm not going to beat about the bush, Mostyn,' said the Old Man, pouring liberal doses of Chivas Regal and pushing a box of panatellas across the desk. 'I'm worried. Dead worried.'

'I should think so too. I'm not feeling particularly perky about things myself.'

'Well? What do you think of the mess?'

'I've only just got back, sir, give me a chance. I've hardly had time to scan the top secret appraisal of the situation; but, from what I did see, it looks pretty ropey.'

'Ropey? Ropey? It's bloody disastrous. They've got us by the short and curlies, lad: and we've got to do something about it at the galloping double. Damn it, this thing could lead to another public enquiry. Hell's teeth...' The Chief had formerly been a Rear Admiral, '...this is the eightth time in three years that I have been hauled in front of the PM. To him, to the Press and to most of the half-baked moronic public, this thing stinks like a Turkish tramdriver's jock strap.'

'Yes, sir, but what...' It was no good; the Chief was in full spate:

'Of course we knew about that wretched pilot officer – snotty-nosed little bastard he is: ought to see him, Mostyn, all Brylcreem and no balls: and the fancy-drawers typist, we had her card marked. Known all about them for months, but, as usual, our hands were tied. Couldn't do a blind thing. No evidence. No blasted co-operation from the Service or the Special Branch. Sweet FA. Then the bleeding SB gets a lucky fluke and nabs 'em. Makes us look pretty damn silly, have another spot of whisky.' He drew a deep breath as the glasses were topped up. 'Wouldn't mind so much if this was an isolated case, but it's always happening.'

'If only we had a way of acting without evidence,' murmured Mostyn. Almost sacrilege, he thought, to suggest something which might imperil the sacred red tape.

'Well, that's it, old son. That's just it. I've formulated a plan: Drastic maybe,' ... he shrugged his shoulders, 'distasteful too, I shouldn't wonder, but I can see no alternative.'

'Well, sir?'

'These people under our twenty-four screen: government department lot, embassies, service personnel, boffins and the like – as soon as we get the slightest whiff of trouble, the smallest niff of a serious security risk, then– Snap!' The Chief was nothing if not dramatic. He brought his hand down on to the desk with such force that Mostyn feared for the whisky. 'Snap! We liquidate 'em.'

'We do what?'

'Liquidate 'em. Dispose of 'em, shoot 'em, give 'em the wooden overcoat, the deep six, the perpetual freeze, the big sleep, the chop. You follow the drift?'

'Chief, it's marvellous, but you'd never get official sanction...'

'And who, by the great Lord Harry, is talking about official sanction?'

'But if anyone ... it's against all the principles of the free world?'

'And who, in the name of the four and twenty virgins who came down from Inverness is bothered about principles? Did you have any principles when you were in the field? We've got to dam the flood, Mostyn. It'll cut our security leaks by half, throw their intelligence cells out of gear and, what seems to be of no little importance, it will

46

save some of our fat greasy necks. We're bound to miss one or two; that's all in the game. We'll still be involved in a few scandals – but, with any luck, they won't be at such frequent intervals.'

'What are the Chiefs of Staff going to say?'

'Mostyn, have you not got it yet?' He sighed, then slowly, as though speaking to a child, continued: 'We are not going to tell the bleeding Chiefs of Staff, nor the blasted PM, nor the adulterous Home Office, nor the sodding Foreign Office. And, particularly, we are not going to tell the fornicating Special Branch. As far as we are concerned, this is to be treated as an internal problem. An entirely domestic affair. No one need know about it except you, myself and the chappie you put on the job. All your boys need know is that we have some kind of 'heavy' working for us – you can give him a fancy designation: "L" for Liquidator something like that. We correlate the evidence and you decide if the button is to be pressed; if you follow me.'

'I don't think any of my boys will be terribly happy about taking on this one, sir. I mean, well, without evidence ... it's tantamount to murder...'

'Then get a murderer.'

Mostyn had to agree that it was a sound idea.

'You can pay him reasonably well. We can

cover that all right. Buy him. Four or five thousand a year should get a decent fellow – mind you, we don't want any of your Soho tearaways, or a bloke who's just missed getting topped. Train a chap if you've got to, but make sure he's loyal. What is the price for loyalty these days, by the way? I'm out of touch.'

'Oh, with the right man, about four thousand or so a year; a flat and a car. Perhaps a little side arrangement – women and that sort of thing.'

'Right. Get cracking. I don't want to hear any more about it. What I want is results!'

As Mostyn reached the door, the Chief added: 'And for heaven's sake, old son, make sure the deaths – when they have to occur – are accidental; we don't want this thing backfiring, do we? Good luck, Mostyn, I'm sure you'll manage everything very nicely.'

Mostyn left the Chief's office with his brain rotating like a small whirlpool. The first reaction was to look among his own men for a suitable applicant for the post of private executioner. Then, as he walked through the General Information Room, fate took a decisive hand.

The GIR in the Department's HQ provides a round-the-clock service for the whole organisation. Here you can follow not only the major political and military global developments, but also trace and check on their smallest repercussions in any given country – even in practically any given town.

It is a long, narrow, uncarpeted room – a subsidiary to the Central Control and Operations Room. At the far end, a great kidney-shaped desk, double-banked with telephones, is staffed by six men who sit – not unlike sub-editors in a Press office – sorting and tabulating information. Behind them, three teletype machines are lovingly tended by a trio of young women. The atmosphere is, paradoxically, one of calm tension. No one speaks above a whisper and, as the telephones work on the winking-light system, the only obvious noise comes from the teletypes as they stutter out their endless paper belt of facts.

The room is divided by a half-wall of filing cabinets. On the right, the long wall is lined with Perspex-covered maps, the other holds a massive blackboard. In front of this stands the 'Newspaper Table' – a plain polished wooden oblong which stretches almost the entire length of the room, with sunken well-desks set into it at every four feet. At the desks an expert crew of three men and four women read, mark, cut and file from every single newspaper, magazine and periodical published throughout the world. A First Class Honours Degree is the minimum requirement for membership of the 'Newspaper Table' crew, and four of its team, at that time, had graduated from erudite fellowships at the senior universities.

As Mostyn came to the end of the 'Newspaper Table', he casually glanced down at the publication lying on top of the stack of newly delivered British provincial weeklies. There, on the front page, staring back at him, framed in newsprint, was the face of Sgt Brian Ian Oakes. He grabbed the paper. The photograph showed Boysie – serious and sober-suited – coming down some steps. It was captioned:

Mr Brian Oakes leaving the Town Hall after Monday's inquest on his partner, Mr Philip Redfern.

There was an inset picture of the late Mr Redfern: a plump gentleman of about forty: bald and smiling soupily. Mostyn pulled up a chair, nodded at the distinctly voluptuous oriental girl who was intent on working her way through the maze of hieroglyphics in a set of Chinese broadcasts, and read the news item. It was headlined:

CAFÉ PROPRIETOR'S DEATH
Partner tells of fall from loft

At an inquest held in the Town Hall on Monday, the Coroner, Mr J.B Hepstall pronounced a verdict of death by misadventure on Philip William Redfern (41), co-owner of the Bird Sanctuary Café and Aviary, Bolney Road. Mr Redfern died on Saturday after an accident at the café – a popular weekend haunt for many local families.

Mr Brian Ian Oakes said that on Saturday evening he went with Redfern to help clear boxes from the garage loft adjoining the café. Redfern started to climb the ladder to the loft when Mr Oakes was called back to the café. Returning a few minutes later he found his partner lying badly injured on the garage floor.

Dr A.H Anderson said that Redfern had died as the result of a fractured skull and brain haemorrhage. 'He obviously slipped as he was pulling himself through the trapdoor,' said Dr Anderson.

Mr Redfern, a keen ornithologist – there are over 600 birds in the Bird Sanctuary Aviary – came to the town, with his wife, in 1946. He took over the old Timber Trees café and converted it into the Bird Sanctuary, in partnership with Mr Oakes, in 1947. Mrs Redfern died in a tragic motor accident last year.

Mr Oakes told *The Gazette:* 'This has been a great shock. Philip Redfern and I were in the army together. I will probably sell the business.'

Mostyn read the paper twice – the paper

came from the Horsham area. He had almost forgotten about Boysie and the Paris incident, but now it was back, lucid with detail. He could see the two corpses and Oakes standing over them: those eyes like pools of ice-chips, and the mouth twisted in a grim smile. If ever there is a compulsive killer, it's this joker, he thought. Now I wonder? The idea was more than just a gleam in the back of his mind. He remembered thinking – in Paris – that Boysie might be useful one day: come to that, he still had a small file on him. It would be interesting to know how the old Army buddy, Redfern, had really died. Even more interesting to know about poor Mrs Redfern.

Back in his office, he rang the Chief:

'I think I might just possibly have a taker for your little scheme,' he said.

'Your little scheme, old Mostyn,' chivvied the Chief. 'It's all yours now, you know. You are on your own.' Mostyn knew exactly what he meant: for a second, the cloud of responsibility passed over his damp brow.

'My little scheme then. OK. The only thing is that I would like to run a trace on him. Can you spare me for a while? I would prefer to do it myself.'

'Take all the time you want. Take a week.'

'Only a week?'

'Only a week.'

'All right. But I'll need Special Branch

cover and no questions asked.'

'I'll fix it.'

'Do you think they'll play?'

'They'd better, after all the trouble they've caused us; and if they won't then I'll cancel the Department's subscription to their bloody Dependants' Fund.'

On the following morning, armed with a Special Branch warrant card, Mostyn turned his silver-grey Bentley on to the A24 out of London and aimed it in the direction of Horsham. During the next few days, he covered a lot of ground: going west to Salisbury, then down to the Dorset coast, into the land of Lulworth Cove and windy Portland Bill. Finally, he motored up through Swindon and Shrivenham into the Vale of the White Horse, under the scarred downs of which Boysie Oakes had taken his first small lungful of air.

He examined police records and dug into files long closed and forgotten. He chatted in public houses, visited Army camps, talked to retired servicemen and gossiped with the school contemporaries of Brian Ian Oakes. By Thursday evening he was back in London – a walking authority on his proposed recruit. He had learned how Boysie was a lad for the ladies; how he had lost his first job through some intriguing hanky-panky with a typist; he heard conflicting reports about his Service career; listened to stories about his relationship with the Redferns – especially a load of malicious stuff about Mrs Redfern, a strapping blonde whose drinking habits had ended in skid marks at midnight. He discovered that the Bird Sanctuary Café and Aviary had been in a definite state of moult for three years, and that Boysie was pressed for cash. Using all the tricks he knew, Mostyn became possessor of a hundred tit-bits of spicy chatter culled from sources official and unofficial, trustworthy and dubious.

His expenses for the trip totalled £56 16s 7d. and, on his return, despite the mine of information, he had gleaned not one shred of evidence linking Boysie with the obsessional blood-lust he had perceived in the alley off the Boulevard Magenta. Both the Redferns had died accidentally, and throughout his life Boysie had not once been associated with any suspicious incident. Yet Mostyn never made mistakes. Boysie, he knew, was a born death-merchant. He had seen too many of them to be wrong. Now he would play it by ear: a few hints just to let Boysie know that his past was an open book to the Department, and the lad would come running. He would not, said Mostyn confidently, be able to resist the temptation to kill again – legally.

So, on the Friday morning, he drove once more to Horsham, turned off down the A281 and arrived at noon in front of the

Bird Sanctuary. Boysie, he was pleased to note, recognised him at once but refused, at first, to be drawn into any conversation about the Paris business. The interview lasted exactly one hour. Mostyn still smiled when he thought about it. There was no doubt that Boysie was a first-class actor. For half the time, he pretended that he did not even understand what Mostyn was getting at. But, when the full implications of the job – with its £4,000 a year, and the flat, and the car – were made known, he had bitten like a well-hooked salmon. Since then, in the whole of their relationship, neither Mostyn nor Boysie had mentioned either the past or Boysie's delight in death. But Mostyn knew and, more important, he knew that Boysie knew.

Within a month, the Bird Sactuary had been sold, and Boysie was safely tucked away in the old Hampshire manor house which is, to the general public, the GPO Executive Training Centre. Those privy to the world of secrets know it, of course, as the most exclusive espionage academy in the world.

The official security check, which had to be made in spite of Mostyn's preliminary investigation, turned up nothing new. Boysie – on a special course, mainly consisting of weapon training, close combat and silent kills – did well. Each week Mostyn grinned happily at the confidential report which landed on his Monday morning desk. But Boysie was essentially a countryman, basically as unsophisticated as a wolf cub, and as gauche as a deb. He was a crack shot, strong and healthy; but Mostyn wanted more than this, and after three months at the Training Centre, he brought his protégé to London for a long, arduous period of grooming and polishing.

To Mostyn, Boysie was a challenge. He would have to be able to go anywhere, with anybody. So, for nine months – using a dozen experts who were at the constant disposal of the organisation – he preened and pruned him: set him to work on books and plays, wine-lists and music. He ran Boysie from restaurant to concert to private viewing to premiere; to tailors to museums. He even took him down to Stratford-upon-Avon to see Badel's Hamlet and Emlyn Williams' Shylock. A noted speech consultant, whose clientele includes royalty, actors and statesmen, spent eight hours a month with him. The chef and *maitre d'hotel* of one of London's most fashionable and exclusive hotels spent over three hours a week with him for three months. One of the leading Sunday drama critics was engaged to give a series of informal lectures on Drama; a professor from the Royal Academy of Music prescribed a course of reading and listening, and an international art expert gave a week of his valuable time.

Mostyn personally supervised Boysie's reading – which ranged from Cervantes and Luther to Murdoch, Amis and Ian Fleming. For weeks, Boysie was marched round the National Gallery, the Natural History Museum, the Horniman Museum, the Tate, the Victoria and Albert and the Wallace Collection. Between times he took short record courses in seven languages – never becoming the least proficient in one. Mostyn had indeed given him the full Pygmalion treatment. A good deal of the crammed culture went right over Boysie's head. But some stuck, and almost a year, to the very day, after the interview in the Bird Sanctuary, Boysie was ready – a tolerable man-about-town with a smattering of small talk, a moderate taste and a veneer of sophistication, set up in the flat behind Chesham Place and waiting for work. Even at that early stage, Mostyn began to worry – which was not surprising when one considered that he had, by now, accepted complete responsibility for both Boysie and the whole dangerous plan.

A month later, a civilian woman clerk from the War Office fell tragically to her death at Surbiton Station – the down line. Then there was the Embassy official in Beirut who seemed to have shot himself in the narrow doorway of a notorious brothel; the Naval officer found drowned at Portsmouth; the poor little filing clerk from the Admiralty who walked under a bus at Gerrards Cross, and the laboratory assistant who...

The knocking on the door shook Mostyn from his nostalgia. It was Big Bertha with Iris's file. He read through it – twice. Nothing there. Age twenty-five. Daughter of a Glaswegian doctor who had moved south in the late thirties. No political affiliations. Joined the Department in 1957 as a junior. Checked all the way through. Grade 1 Schedule two years ago. Mostyn's personal secretary for the last twelve months, so subject to the monthly check. Last check: Security Rating A1.

Nothing that he didn't already know: she was as clean and well-screened as anybody else in the Department. But something was bothering Mostyn – and it wasn't just the fact that Iris and Boysie had infringed that blasted regulation. The tick in his mind was jumping overtime.

He picked up the list of security alerts for the following week. First trials of a new anti-submarine device at Portland on Monday afternoon; the Duke's visit to RAF Gay-borough on Tuesday morning (he paused over this one, it was marked Top Secret Priority and there was an embargo on newspapers until after the visit); on Wednesday the Russian Ambassador was being taken round an aircraft factory in Coventry, with a visit to the cathedral later in the day. Nothing spectacular.

Still something clicked in his mind. Anyway, that afternoon, he would ring the love-birds in their little sunlit nest and put the fear of God into them. Until then, better be safe than out of a job. He dialled the Operations Room:

'Operations – Captain Blair.'

'Number Two here, Blair. Tell me, who *is* our man on the Côte D'Azur?'

3 – *CÔTE D'AZUR*

Saturday June 8th 1963

SHERIEK

High over the Alps, power was reduced: the inner engines of the Comet brought back to idling in preparation for the long, gentle let-down that would bring the flight to an end in front of the 'Arrivals' building of the Nice Terminal. Coming out over the sea, the Captain selected twenty degrees of flap, and the aircraft descended in a wide steady turn, to line up with the grey wave-washed runway.

Looking down the tilted wing, one could see nearly the whole craggy coastline – Italy in the distance veiled in a scorching haze. The sheltering mountains, massive buttresses against the horizon, stretched severely up from the water, jagged patterns against the endless blue of sky: their detail crisp, and textures vivid, in the afternoon air – savage fascias of rock: boulders light against the dark green of conifer and foliage. Below them, leaning on the foot-hills and poised around the bays, sprawled the seaboard towns: built between clusters of eucalyptus, orange, lemon and palm: their buildings sharp – angles of terra-cotta, cream, pink and mud-grey – glistening in the brilliant sun.

The sea was so clear that, as the aircraft lost height, one could pick out the inshore rocks drowned in a honeycomb of wave-shadows; dots of foam from the bathers scattered across the surface, and the thin, white, bubbling surf spreading and clearing in flat, uneven ribbons.

The undercarriage was down: flaps at sixty degrees: rpm 6,000. The runway lay dead ahead – heat leaping up from the hard surface, giving a shimmer of perpetual motion to the low air.

Sitting on the terrace of the airport restaurant, Sheriek and the girl sipped their *Curaçao* – the *coup de grace* to a light lunch of *Quenelles de Sole* and *salade vert*.

Sheriek was a smooth man: a unique creation from a cosmopolitan mixing bowl. His mother had been a Eurasian harlot, in her day the favourite of a plush brothel in Cannes; his father, the result of a sharp, sweet alliance between a Russian officer and Flamenco. Such a co-mingling of races had left its mark. The dark eyes, healthy black hair and perfect teeth came from his father's side; while his mother had provided the high cheek bones, long flat nose, thick lips and olive complexion.

For fifty years – from the age of four – Sheriek had plied many cryptic and often highly lucrative trades up and down the playground coast. Now, feeling the first real onset of age, he was often conscious of a burdening sense of failure. To satisfy, his life needed some grand coup on which he could look back with pleasure in old age.

Sheriek had tried often and hard – perhaps too hard – to grasp at his ambition. In his time, he had spied for at least five nations – including France, who had short-sightedly paid him off with a Croix de Guerre, the ribbon of which he wore discreetly in his buttonhole: a warning to any gendarme who might be tempted to question him about some minor offence.

In his dreams, he saw himself as a Master Agent: a Spy Supreme with the destiny of kingdoms between his fists. In reality, he knew that he was only a very small wheel in a huge mechanism which, if he slipped out of place, would crush him as mercilessly as he, himself, would swat an insect. With this revelation there also came a deeper per-ception of the increasing downhill speed of advancing time. Hence, the beautiful hands – immaculately manicured and heavy with gold – with which he constantly caressed his person: feeling his arms and shoulders, running a palm up his heavy thighs, or the base of a thumb across his chest: letting his fingers glide along his forehead, over his cheek and around his chin to trickle down the neck. The movements had become predictable, habitual, as though to reassure him that the flesh and bone were still there, intact and, as yet, undecayed. For the same reason, he seldom appeared in public without a girl – preferably ostentatiously sexy: proof to the world that his physical appetite remained untarnished.

The Comet's engines dropped to a low whine as it settled safely on to the concrete: then with a giant snarl – motors reversed to slow the landing – it rolled, braking smoothly, to the end of the runway. Sheriek leaned forward and patted the girl's hand:

'Now. I think it is time to leave, my dear. Let us go and see if he is anything like his pretty picture.'

'Ow! Do we have to go *now?* I like it here.' The girl was English: a snatch of Maida Vale interlaced with West Kensington. She pouted prettily.

'Come along.' Sheriek was stroking the hand, as though willing some of its youth to rub off on his experienced fingers. 'The sooner we go, the sooner we get this job over, and the sooner there will be lots of money for you to buy all the little things you so want. Eh?'

The girl turned her head to look at the big metal bird moving in towards the Terminal

Building. With a rattling grumble, a Super Constellation of uncertain age trundled down the runway and took off – far too steeply – with a black trail of exhaust streaming from its port inner. Adjusting her sunglasses, the girl rose from her chair – straining upwards like a lazy cat, so that the whole of her precise body pressed outwards against her clothes in one exotic ripple. There was a sharp intake of breath from Sheriek. The girl shot him a sunbeam smile:

'Come on then, Sherry love, what are we waiting for? Lead me to him.'

As they moved through the restaurant, several forks were arrested between plates and mouths, while eyes followed the girl's buttocks, rotating like a pair of small, well-balanced grindstones set and perfectly harmonised on slender legs.

The couple crossed the foyer, and stationed themselves behind the knot of taxi men, hotel bus drivers and friends waiting to greet the sun-seekers newly arrived from Britain. A cluster of all-in, first-time, never-had-it-so-good tourists (like glum sheep) straggled past them into the transit lounge; murmuring against oily food, mosquitoes, the heat, warm Guinness and the prices; whishing they had returned yet again to Clacton, Margate or merry Morecambe.

Sheriek, his eyes focused on the small, metal-fenced entrance through which the

Riviera pilgrims would have to come, opened his copy of *Paris Match*. On the right-hand centre page, he had cellotaped a photograph: Boysie smiled jauntily at him, stuck firmly over the navel and chest of a muscular young woman in sequined briefs.

Sheriek glanced down to re-familiarise himself with the face. The passengers were beginning to dribble into the foyer now: a tall man lugging two vast cases, followed by a thin woman with a testy infant; a studious young man clutching a paper-back Kafka; a grande dame loudly goading a sweating porter who bent visibly under what seemed to be three small cabin trunks and an out-size hat-box; two girls, all confidence and desperately Marshall and Snelgrove; a man … a man… Sheriek's eyes narrowed:

'That's him, my baby. That's our boy,' he hissed.

'Mm, is *that* him?' said the girl, all velvet. 'He's dishy.'

Sheriek took her arm, spun her round, and marched her quickly through the big swing doors, out into the sun and over to the black and white Lincoln Continental parked strategically with a view of the Terminal's frontage.

'There should be a woman,' he said, turning on the ignition. 'They told me there would be a woman. We'll just make sure: then I think we can afford to race him home.

And after that, my dear, it will be up to you.'

'He really is dishy,' said the girl, opening her compact and scrutinising a pair of temptingly arranged lips. 'Really dishy.'

Boysie stepped out of the entrance hall, breathed a silent prayer of thanksgiving for his safe return to earth, lit a cigarette, and allowed his nostrils to take in a generous measure of Riviera air.

Odd, how quickly one forgot the particular smell of places. London had a scent all of her own; and Paris: but now he couldn't recall either. Here, along the Blue Coast, it was a subtle blend of baked earth, *Ambre Solaire,* naked sea-coated bodies, raw spirits, strong tobacco, new bread, the rough red *Côte de Provence,* with a nose-wrinkle of garlic to complete the bouquet. It was a redolence exclusive to the Côte D'Azure.

'Taxi, monsieur?' The fat, glistening driver was motioning him towards a minute Renault.

'Oui...' Boysie struggled for the right words. 'Oui ... un moment...' The man scooped the Revelation from his feet and began to strap it to the roof rack.

'Montez, monsieur.' He paused, then added in an uncertain accent, 'Where you go?'

'Menton.'

'Ah, oui, monsieur, Menton. Montez, Montez.'

'Un moment ... er ... une fille ... ma femme... Oh, how the hell do you say "I am waiting for my wife"?'

'J'attends ma femme.' The voice was husky in his ear.

Iris stood behind him, one leg thrust forward, bent at the knee, so that the gentle curve of her thigh showed smooth against the black capeskin shift dress. Her military-styled raincoat, casually thrown across her shoulders, gave an impression of studied elegance: the whole line of her body erect – almost arrogant. Below a high forehead, large brown eyes – rimmed by striking feathery lashes – looked out in a penetrating stare as though she searched for some undiscovered facet in the world around her. For a couple of seconds, the look – aimed steadily at Boysie – touched insolence; then her mouth, full to the point of petulance, spread into an open grin, softening her features and revealing a warmth not apparent when her face was in sophisticated repose.

To Boysie, she was exquisite: from the tips of her patent cut-away court shoes to the final strands of upswept hair – the colour of polished copper.

Apart from the language difficulty, Boysie had just about regained the poise lost on the outward flight. The arrival of Iris, at this moment in his linguistic battle, should, by rights, have knocked him off balance: even humiliated him. But, so pleased was he to see her, that it took a genuine effort of will not to disclose both his heartfelt thanks for her interruption, and his urgent physical joy at being close to her once more. For a fraction, he gawped like a schoolboy, then, as though drawing on a mantle of maturity, he gave her a relaxed, highly quizzical smile:

'Jolly good. We made it then. Marvellous,' he drawled, in a manner so like Mostyn's that she could have slapped his face.

The taxi man whipped up her case, banging it next to the Revelation on the roof. Boysie opened the door, pushed the driver's seat forward, and helped Iris into the back of the car, letting his eyes drop to take in the quick stretch of nylon-sheathed knee and thigh, visible as her skirt rode back in the awkward jostle of settling into the machine's tiny interior. Boysie prised himself in beside her, still slyly eyeing the knees. She squeezed his hand:

'Don't look so lascivious, darling.'

'Sorry, sweetie, but it's quite a view.'

Iris giggled, pulling at the shiny hem of her dress in a vain attempt at mock-modesty.

'Glad you came?' asked Boysie, nuzzling her ear.

'I'll tell you in the morning.' She paused; then, looking straight at him, unsmiling: 'Poor Boysie, I've kept you on a string for such a long time, haven't I? Never mind, darling, I'll do my best to make it a memorable weekend.'

Boysie reflected that he had never known Iris in such a coming-on mood. All her reticence, the half-promises, the guarded answers and the uncertainty – which had existed even up to last night – were gone; a kind of sensual confidence taking their place.

The large driver loaded himself into the front of the car, and with much grating of gears, they pulled away from the kerb at a speed which would not have been out of place on the Nurburgring. Horn blaring, they shaved the back of a small 'Correspondence' bus and set off towards the Promenade des Anglais.

'À Menton!' shouted the driver, as though issuing an order to his vehicle. At the same time, he turned on the radio with a flourish, as if to show his passengers that the service provided almost all mod. cons.

'Why do I always have to pick "characters"?' asked Boysie, closing his eyes as the Renault slid within half an inch of a motor scooter.

'You have the consolation of knowing that he is probably thinking exactly the same thing,' said Iris, patting his arm.

The car was filled by a violent gust of music, followed by what sounded like a stream of Gallic obscenities. The announcer was doing a commercial for a sparkling cordial which rejoices in the uncommon trade name of *Pschitt!* By the time they came abreast of the snooty Hotel Negresco, the word had been repeated at regular intervals in the ad. man's script and Iris was spluttering into her handkerchief.

'Ooh, en't he coarse,' she mimicked in a soppy-date voice.

Boysie, cackling happily, leant over and kissed her ear – briefly catching a trace of the *Guerlain Chant D'Aromes* which he had bought her last week in Bond Street.

As they turned on to the littoral road which hugs the twisting coastline, rising from Nice to Menton, the big black and white Continental shot past them with a high-volume horn blast and a swirl of dust. Boysie did not even notice: he was engrossed in running the third finger of his left hand up and down the inside of Iris' forearm – the raincoat now pushed back to show the crisp white nylon blouse which she wore under the shift.

'Did you enjoy the flight, darling?' said Iris, the throatiness conveying her increasing sexual preparedness.

'Bit of a bore, really,' said Boysie, still hard at work on the erogenetic area on the crook of her elbow.

The red-canopied Royal Bar – favourite post-prandial haunt of tourists – stands immediately adjacent to the aloof, brass-plated Hotel Miramont, half-way up Menton's Avenue de Verdun. Commercially its site is perfect: only a minute from the ritzy Casino and Sporting Club, and directly opposite the palm and cacti dotted Jardin Bioves.

The Continental drew up at the farthest extremity of the Royal's maze of tables. Sheriek stopped the motor and turned to the girl:

'Here we are, my dear. You are certain you know what to do?'

She nodded, resigned and bored in the oppressive heat which slewed up from the road and off the tall buildings. She would rather have been going down to the rocky private plage at Beaulieu to wash away the sunsweat and mid-afternoon lassitude.

Sheriek purred on, his hand clamped possessively just above her knee:

'If you have had no opportunity by six o'clock, then I will come back and we will have to use my other plan. Until then, I will be waiting with the car. And be a good girl, my dear: do not ogle the men.'

'I never ogle, Sherry darling. I can't help it if I have sexy eyes.'

She wrenched her knee from his hand and jumped out of the car. Waving to Sheriek, she walked the few paces to the Royal and sat down at the first table. Ordering a café noir and a packet of Gitanes, she began the vigil.

Twenty minutes later, she saw the Renault pull up, and watched, from behind diamante-framed sunglasses, as Boysie and Iris were ushered through the twirling doors of the Miramont. With what those two seem to have in mind, it looks like I'm in for a long wait, she thought. Stirring her third cup of coffee, she realised that she was just a little jealous of the slim, graceful red-head who had accompanied her quarry into the hotel.

The air-conditioned freshness of the Miramont's entrance hall came as a relief after the hot, dusty drive from Nice. Feeling up to their knees in carpet, and preceded by a small page-boy (who humped the two cases with considerable determination), Boysie and Iris crossed to the reception desk. Despite careful grooming before leaving London, both were now conscious of being travel-crumpled as they moved among the lacquered, pressed and coiffured atmosphere of stealthy servants and luxury-class clientele. There was the ritual of register-signing – Boysie, with a slow smile, captivating the petite receptionist – (He never stops – talk about acrobats! thought Iris, a shade testy) – then the swift elevator ride and the pad along silent corridors.

'Boysie, this is fab, just fab,' said Iris – spinning, with arms outstretched – in the centre of the room: taking in the pearl décor, the flowers, the fluttering ninon curtains, wide balcony and the whole sheer expensive feel of the boudoir. Her almost girlish enthusiasm was something new to Boysie:

'I thought the bridal suite would be appropriate.'

'Oh no! Boysie, you didn't.' Iris cannoned into the bed and ended, bouncing, on the heavy white satin coverlet. 'Boysie, you swine: that was why we got all those dreadful looks from the staff.'

With the speed of a cheetah at full tilt, he was across the room and beside her on the bed.

'Well,' he said, as though it summed up the whole situation.

She leaned back: hair gleaming against the shiny fabric. Boysie put one hand under her neck and lowered his face to hers. She responded: then, as though suddenly remembering something, pulled away from him.

'Give me a chance, darling. You're too eager.'

Boysie tried again.

'No, Boysie. Please; not yet. I feel filthy – even travelling by air. Let me get ... adjusted. Later, I promise.'

Boysie raised himself on one elbow and kissed her nose

74

'If that's how the biscuit breaks, sweetie.'

They looked at each other. Iris frowned:

'Why have you taken so much trouble with me, Boysie? I mean, there must be plenty of other girls…'

'There are plenty of other girls.' His conceit infuriated her.

'Then why bother? All the time and energy you've spent – and money.'

'Why does any man? The mystery of that which is denied – as they say?'

'They also say that the greatest passion is the one that is never consummated.'

'Nuts to that. I have a *thing* about you, Iris – that's all there is to it.'

'And I have a *thing* about you, Boysie. Give me a cigarette.'

He took out his case, opening it to show the symmetrical cork-coloured row of king-sized filters:

'Oh, not one of those. They're cheats. If you're going to dice with death, you should do it properly. Away with filters! At this very moment there are probably little pickets of germs marching round your epiglottis with signboards saying "Ban the Filter" and "Unfair to Cancer".'

She got off the bed – another slice of leg. Boysie reflexed – a hand moving out to her: then, remembering, he pulled back. Iris again began to twirl around the room in a sort of schoolgirl joydance. It puzzled Boysie; he was discovering hidden shallows in Iris.

'I'm in France. I'm having a naughty weekend with a very attractive man (What *would* Mummy say?) Tonight I want to dine on – what? *Terrine de Canard a l'Orange...?*' She was acting outrageously. Excited? A little afraid?

('You'll get steak, eggs and chips, mate, and like it,' grunted Boysie.)

'...And now I want to smoke strong, strong, Blue Gauloises.'

'Okay, I'll ring down.'

'Oh, Boysie,' disappointed.

'What's wrong now?'

'Look, love, can't you see? I want you out of the way for a while – little feminine repairs and unpacking. Be a dear: nip out and get me some Gauloises. Just for a few minutes.' She wheedled: 'Please, Boysie. Pretty please.'

He put his arm round her shoulders, squeezed her and lodged a smacking kiss on her cheek:

'Okay, me old darlin'. Can I just slip into something loose first?'

'Be my guest.'

He lugged the Revelation into the bath-room: sea-green tiles, inlaid strip-lighting and shiny chrome– 'Not quite my style,' said Boysie to the large, almost symbolic, bidet. He ran the shower, unlocked the case – transferring the pistol and ammunition to the zip pocket on the inside of the lid.

A quarter-of-an-hour later, he emerged, tingling from the shower and changed into spongebag check slacks, white linen shirt and rope-closed sandals. Iris stood on the balcony, looking down into the street, lazy with leggy girls and broad bronzed men.

'How do you like the tout ensemble then?' He turned slowly: a male model in a monthly glossy. Iris walked round him:

'Well the tout looks OK, but I'm not sure about the ensemble.'

'We read the same books, darling,' he said, doing his Noel Coward.

She giggled: 'You look very beautiful, Boysie. Now what about my fags?'

'Six packets of Gauloises Bleu coming up,' said Boysie. 'Then, I think, dinner at the fabulous Sporting Club, a quick whirl at the tables, followed by...?' He arched his eyebrows.

'Oh, get out.' She smiled: then, softly: 'I'll be waiting for you, Boysie.'

In the street, he put on his sunglasses, lit a cigarette, and walked past the Royal to the corner opposite the Casino. Crossing the road, he turned and stood looking back at the uneven view of peaks behind the Jardins Bioves. The backdrop mountains were beginning to change colour, sharp in the still air – the sky now milky-blue behind them. He glanced at his watch. Four forty-five.

Boysie sauntered through the crowds and bought the cigarettes at the bar tabac in the Place St Roche, among a press of postcard-hunting English girls, and walked on to the seafront. The rocks and pebble beaches were jigsawed with bodies catching the day's last sun. He thought of Iris and tomorrow. By then, the first flush of pleasure would be over and they could lie satiated among the water-smoothed stones, or play, giddy, in the surf. Perhaps, by then, he would be free from his obsession with her – this illogical, immature thing that had hounded him for half a year, even when he was with other women. Unaccountably, his mind changed direction, becoming focused on Mostyn – now there was an obsessional character if you like. Suddenly depressed, he began the return journey to the hotel.

It happened as he was turning back into the Avenue Verdun. The girl came round the corner walking at speed. Boysie, not really looking where he was going, tried to twist his lean body out of the way; but it was too late: their shoulders met with a bruising jar. He made a grab for her, but the force of the collision, combined with the girl's forward velocity, sent her careening into the wall. She gave a little cry and ended in a dainty heap his feet.

'I'm sorry... Pardon, madame ... er made-moiselle...'

'Oh, you're English! Oh!'

She was blonde: twentyish: short, and poured into oyster silk pants and shirt. A spotted silk bandana was knotted at her throat below a cheeky elfin face, topped by splendid gold hair which curled under the nape of her neck, just touching the ears. Boysie could smell the sun on her flesh as he helped her to her feet, noting, with pleasure, the firm contours tight against her second skin of clothes – the grapefruit breasts and the telltale curved-V elastic line of her panties showing clear up the rounded bottom.

'Ooh!' She grimaced, gently pawing the pavement with her right foot.

'You all right?' said Boysie.

'I'm not sure.' She smiled through a wince of pain. 'It's my ankle. I twisted it when I fell. Must have sprained it. Ooh, damn!'

'Bad?'

'Not too good. Making me feel sick.' She was pale under the berry-brown tan: leaning against the wall.

'Think you ought to see a doctor?'

'If I can get back to the hotel, I'll be all right. Daddy will know what to do.'

'Where's the hotel? And Daddy?'

'Up in Garavan; not far; in the Old Town. Ouch: crumbs, this is painful.'

'Crumbs' was not the kind of expletive Boysie expected from this sort of girl.

'Well, let me help. After all, I knocked you over.'

'Oh, it was my fault... But ... well ... if I could hold your arm ... I think I might manage to get to the car.' She pointed across the Gardens. 'It's over there: in one of those side streets.'

'OK. You're sure you're going to be all right?' She nodded, biting her lip. Game little bird, thought Boysie.

'Let's go then.' She took a few tentative, hobbling, steps clutching at his forearm.

'Look,' said Boysie, as they reached the low hooped fence which separated the Gardens from the pavement, 'wouldn't it be better like this?' He curled his arm round her comfortable yielding waist.

'Ooh, yes!' said the girl, allowing herself to be pulled closer. 'I say, aren't you strong?'

The car was parked in a narrow cobbled alley, flanked by high red-washed irregular buildings which looked as though they had been designed by a romantic, sun-struck alcoholic. She slid into the driving seat and tested her damaged foot on the pedals.

'The wretched thing is swelling. D'you know, I don't think I'm going to be able to drive.'

'Come on then, move over.'

'Oh, you angel! Would you? Would you really? You are being kind. Are you sure?'

Boysie, doing a quick check to familiarise

himself with the controls, had just reached out for the starter when he sensed the danger from behind. Half-turning, he glimpsed a raised arm. The girl gave a yelp, and something flashed across his eyes. A circle of stars and four new planets shot into orbit round his skull. Then Boysie Oakes fell on to the steering wheel and into deep, thick darkness.

Boysie had been gone for about five minutes when the telephone rang. Iris, dressed only in lacy bra and briefs, turned from her unpacking and lifted the receiver:

'Hullo?'

'Telephone pour Monsieur ou Madame Oakes.'

'Oui.' Boysie at one of his pranks again, thought Iris. There was a wave of static and then a voice clear in her ear:

'Hullo.'

'Hullo?'

'Is that Mrs Oakes?'

'Who is that?'

'Iris, I'm so glad I've caught you in. It's your old uncle Mostyn. Just ringing to see how you're getting on. You should have let me know you were spending the weekend with your husband.'

'How the...?'

'I have my spies everywhere, lovey, you should know that.'

Iris used a four-letter word much favoured

by licentious soldiery, D.H Lawrence, sick comedians and beat novelists.

'So I should imagine,' said Mostyn, grinning far away in drab Whitehall.

4 – *CÔTE D'AZUR*

Saturday June 8th 1963

CORAL

A dozen little green men, shod in steel-capped boots, were punctiliously kicking their way out of Boysie's skull. He imagined that he could see them through the crimson-wash of cloud which sifted behind his eyes.

He was the inside of his head. There was nothing else. All feeling and being had somehow reduced itself to a huge blood-filled cranium. And that was him: inside.

Far away someone was groaning. Then a voice began whispering down a narrow tunnel, and he felt something deliciously cool on the desert of forehead. With the coolness, sensation began to return. The whisper got louder. A woman's voice:

'Are you all right? There, there, there now.' It was the sound of a mother soothing a fallen child. For what seemed like an age, Boysie was back in his childhood village under the Berkshire Downs – Ma comforting, because he had grazed a knee playing 'chain-tig' in the lane. The head shrunk. It was equipped with a neck. There were shoulders, and arms, and a torso, and – a long way off – feet.

He braced himself and heaved open his eyes. Somewhere above him swimming like an image in a mobile distorting mirror, was the face of a blonde. His lids snapped shut, then opened again. This time he held on until normal vision returned. The world swung in two great circles: the blonde's face did a series of gentle revolves, and things began to settle into a recognisable pattern. The girl looked worried, and he discovered that the cool thing on his forehead was her hand, gently brushing and smoothing:

'Oh, thank heaven, you're all right. I thought you were never going to wake up. Now lie still. Don't try and sit up.' She put a restraining hand on his shoulder.

'What happened?' said Boysie, foolishly. His mouth seemed to be full of a foul-tasting brand of cotton wool.

'Someone hit you.'

'Oh.'

'On the back of the head.'

'Why?'

'I don't know.' The girl seemed a trifle piqued. 'I was hoping *you'd* tell *me.*'

'Well, where am I … are we?' He sat up, wished he hadn't, and was forced to cling to the side of the bed until the room stopped doing its realistic imitation of a switchback.

'I don't know. It's a kind of cellar. They brought us down steps, I know: I could feel them.'

Boysie felt both angry and frightened:

'Look, what the hell's going on?' He put his hand to his head and felt it cautiously. Just above the right ear a swelling, the size of a small plum, throbbed painfully.

'I think we've been kidnapped,' said the girl in the breathless confidential tone of a sixth-former announcing – at the school dance – that her suspender has snapped. 'The pointed a gun at me and stuck a needle in your arm – you know, injection thing...'

Instinctively, he felt above his elbows. There was a bruised area just below the left shoulder. That accounted for the nauseating taste in his mouth.

'...Then they dumped you into the back of the car, put a horrible smelly sack over my face and told me to lie down...'

'They raped you? The bastards!'

'No, not that kind of lie down – in the back of the car ... so that I couldn't see where we were going.'

Boysie was beginning to remember: Iris, the Miramont, Gauloises, the girl's ankle. He looked at his watch. It was seven-thirty: two and three-quarter hours since he had left Iris.

'How's your ankle?'

'My...? Oh, I'd almost forgotten – they

carried me in here. It doesn't seem too bad. You were kind about that. Thank you.'

'Hasn't done either of us much good, has it?'

'No. I'm sorry.' Then, like a child at a picnic: 'Why have they kidnapped us?'

'I haven't the foggiest idea. Oh, my achin' head.'

Boysie was dead worried. Never, in the whole of his career with the Department, had anything like this happened to him. Ye gods, he thought, what if it *is* me they're after? Up to now, Mostyn had been his only real concern. When his conscience pricked it was because of fear and guilt about facts withheld and his prolonged deception – the wool-pulling over Mostyn's eyes. He had never really considered any danger from the other side. Now it looked as though they had caught up with him. His guts gave a triple forward-roll followed by a couple of nifty bowel-springs. To make it worse, he caught sight of a spider edging its way up the wall. If Boysie had made a long list of all the things he disliked – apart from flying – spiders would have come out pretty near the top. He took a deep, nervous breath (which turned into a shudder) and looked around.

They were in a bare, windowless room – a cell of whitewashed brick. Above, a single light burned from behind a convex grille, sunk into the ceiling. There was no trace of a switch: the walls as naked as the proverbial baby's backside. The door, which seemed to have been carved straight from an overgrown oak, was set flush with the wall – no sign of a lock, or handle, on the inside. The only furniture was the one matressed bed – an iron hospital cot – on which they were sitting. The air felt dry and the temperature was not unpleasantly cool.

He continued to puzzle at the problem. Their attackers had been hiding in the car. A ray of hope: the fact that they were already waiting in the car would mean that they were after the girl and not him at all. He looked at her – ridiculously pert-pretty. Under different circumstances it would have been a pleasure to be locked in a room with her – especially a room which only contained a bed. He was about to ask who the devil she was (some blasted millionaire's daughter, no doubt), when the sound of bolts and chains rattled in from the other side of the door.

Automatically, they both stood up, the blonde slipping her hand into his. The floor weaved slightly.

'Don't worry,' he whispered, trying to control his knees which were striking up a zapateado. She looked at him with helpless, and devastating eyes:

'I won't.' She forced a brave smile.

'By the way,' said Boysie out of the corner of his mouth, 'what's your name?'

'Coral. Isn't it stupid? It's Coral White.'

The door opened and they looked into the nasty end of a Browning .32.

The man with the gun sported the face of a decaying camel: brown, thin, long-jawed and sinister. His companion was obviously a hybrid of the Frankenstein strain: about six feet seven; shoulders like a Henry Moore statue, and a face which Boysie seemed to remember having once seen on a large, unpleasant piece of T'ang Dynasty sculpture – squat, dome-headed, moronic and transcendentally evil. Both wore heavy dark glasses.

Camel-Face looked at the girl:

'You stay.' The accent had vague German connotations.

'You come.' The pistol muzzle moved in a slow, accurate arc from the left side of Boysie's chest to the centre of the door, and back again.

'Good luck,' whispered Coral. He squeezed her hand, swallowed hard, and obeyed: treading, like the biblical Agag, delicately. Frankenstein's cousin stretched out his iron arm and rested a banana-bunch hand on Boysie's shoulder. It was almost a gentle gesture, but the fingers were curled expertly, their tips touching the pressure points on his neck. A tightening of grip would inflict excruciating agony.

Across the threshold, Boysie found himself on a narrow landing – a tiny ante-room draped on three sides with black velvet. The door closed behind them. Darkness. He could feel the hand on his shoulder, hear the heavy breathing and the scrape of bolts being pushed home. Then the gun was in his back:

'Hiep!' It was a parade-ground order, shouted into his ear and accompanied by a two-handed push, smart in the small of the back. Boysie took off and shot, head first, through the curtains into a blinding glare of light. His shin caught something hard, and he came to a stumbling halt, half bent over a chair back.

'Good evening, Mr Oakes. I am so happy you were able to join us.'

The voice came, silky, and disembodied, from behind the battery of lamps. Boysie was standing in the converging beams of five tactically placed theatrical mirror spots. He shaded his eyes, trying to peer through the light, and could just make out a pair of hands at the far end of a polished mahogany table. He had to screw up his eyelids, leaving only tiny slits, to keep out the dazzling brilliance. The cone of light generated a formidable amount of heat, and already he could feel himself sweating.

'Do sit down, Mr Oakes. Make yourself comfortable,' crooned Sheriek, complacent from behind his radiant curtain. Boysie felt his way on to the chair and tried to look around him; but the massed beams cut off his view on both sides. It was, he thought, like a rather high-class third degree room. The Man-Mountain stood to the right of the chair, and he could sense the gun-toter at the back of his neck.

Boysie leaned across the table, straining his eyes:

'Look here,' he said, an irate Englishman done out of his rights. 'What's all this about?' His voice was unsteady, and he could feel control slipping from his lip muscles – a sure sign of fear.

'You do not know what it is all about, Mr Oakes? I should have imagined that, in your profession, one would be constantly prepared for the day of reckoning.'

'I don't know what you're talking about – whatever your name is – but I demand that you release Miss White and myself immediately. My wife is waiting for me at our hotel – she's probably been in touch with the consul already; and as for Miss White...' He dried. It was the best he could think of for the moment.

'Your wife, Mr Oakes? We did not know you had a wife; and I must remind you that you are in no position to demand anything.'

'Well...'

'As you say... Well!'

At this point, Boysie admitted to himself

that he, and not the girl, was the centre of this bizarre plot. Twelve red admirals and a lone cabbage white were doing an enthusiastic ballet in his lower intestine, and sweat – drawn out not by the lights, but through mortal funk – spouted from his pores like a series of chilly fountains.

'Let us put our cards on the table,' resumed Sheriek. 'I apologise for not being able to introduce myself – but I think you would agree that it would reduce the air of mystery. I am a great follower of detective fiction, Mr Oakes; and the more entangled tales of your great espionage writers. I return to the adventures of Mr Richard Hannay with almost the same avidity as I resort to the Bible and the Koran when I am in need of spiritual consolation...'

'That's a bit square, isn't it?' Boysie was surprised at his own cheek. 'Buchan is considered to be in the decline these days.'

'Maybe it is a sign of my age. But as you may yet have an opportunity of finding out, I dip into other books. The works of the Marquis de Sade figure largely among my bedtime favourites.'

'I can imagine.' Boysie was finding it difficult to retain a proper perspective of the affair – it seemed so fantastically melo-dramatic. But the very fact of his own job, and the way in which Mostyn had steam-rollered him into it, always seemed to hover

91

on the borderline of fantasy.

'As I was saying…' In his element, Sheriek was ready to twist the knife. 'I cannot introduce myself. However, you have met Yacob – he is the large gentleman – and Gregory, he carries the gun. I think you will find that he is almost as accurate a shot as yourself.'

'I seldom go shooting.'

'No? I wonder. Let me give you a few facts about yourself, Mr Oakes.' There was a pause. Sheriek cleared his throat. 'Your name is Brian Ian Oakes. You are known to your friends by the slightly ridiculous, and, if you will forgive me for saying so, rather effeminate, nickname – Boysie. Your occupation is hired assassin. As such, you work for the British Department of Special Security – under the code-letter "L". You have been with them for about six, maybe seven, years. In that time, you have personally dispatched twenty-five agents, or suspected agents, occupied in espionage against the United Kingdom.'

This was far worse than the alarming nightmares in which he faced Mostyn over the hard facts of his many dissemblings. *They* had got him now – and not just by the nose either. This was the real end: the terminus of the perishing track.

'Now, Mr Oakes, we are both adult men.' Sheriek was getting nicely into his stride. 'We both know that you are not indispensable to your organisation. Anyone can be replaced, so there is no point in merely killing you. Before we decide what is to be done – and I must tell you quite frankly that your future does not depend on me – I am going to ask you one question.'

'I don't know where you get your information,' Boysie said with total lack of confidence. 'But I've got nothing to do with this Special Whatnot Security thing. You're talking an absolute load of old rubbish...'

'The question,' Sheriek continued, ignoring Boysie's hopeless denial, 'is simply: why are you here?'

Boysie spoke without thinking: 'Because you brought me here, you screaming old nit.' The blow, from the back of Yacob's hand, caught him slap in the centre of the cheek. He picked himself up and groped back on to the chair. The giant's knuckles were like billiard balls.

'We will have no more of that kind of insolence, please, Mr Oakes. I will ask you once more: Why are you in France? Who is your target?'

'Honestly,' Boysie sounded like a boy facing his housemaster, 'I don't know what you're on about. I'm in France for a week-end holiday with a very ... with my wife.'

There was a silence, not so much pregnant as stillborn. Sheriek sighed – a wave of garlic wafted over the table:

'I had hoped to avoid any nastiness. You are a very foolish man, Boysie Oakes.'

Boysie's right-hand fingernails were digging hard into the back of his left hand. For a moment, he did not know where the pain was coming from. The atmosphere was fraught with horrible possibilities, and he had a pretty good idea what the next item on this harrowing programme was going to be.

'You like Miss White?' the question was unexpected.

'Well. I hardly know her. Damn it, I'd only just met the girl about five minutes before your goons jumped me...'

'No, Yacob!' Sheriek's loud command just stopped the gorilla from repeating the backhand treatment.

'But you like her?'

'She's a nice girl. Yes.' The more revolting probabilities of this line of conversation began to filter into Boysie's pounding head:

'Now, look: keep Miss White out of it. She had nothing to do with this: nothing to do with me. Good grief...'

Sheriek smiled amiably to himself. It had been quite a brilliant stroke of subtlety to leave Coral with this man. Now there could be a final appeal to the Britisher's sense of fair play. He looked out, from the safety of his spotlight barricade. Apart from the strangely clear blue eyes, the cringing, undeniably handsome, man on the other side of the table, didn't look at all like a monstrous killer to him. Devilishly clever, these English. Friend Oakes was undoubtedly a talented actor. Sheriek never believed in underrating his opponent:

'Now, I am going to have my dinner. We will return to this matter in roughly...' There was a movement from behind the lights as he looked at his watch. '...In roughly one hour. Then, Mr Oakes, I will again ask you that question–What are you doing in France and whom have you been sent to kill? If you are still not prepared to answer me, we will have to try the ultimate method of persuasion. Would you be so good as to look upwards.'

Boysie obediently raised his eyes. A large metal pulley was screwed hard into the ceiling above his head.

'You have heard of the *strappado*, yes?'

Boysie nodded. It was one of the most simple and effective tortures in the book. The hands, tied behind the back, were attached to a cord which ran through the pulley. You were then hauled upwards and allowed to fall with a jerk which dislocated the shoulder-joints.

'Yacob is most efficient with the *strappado*. He has a rather gay variation of his own.' Yacob moved a little – proud at the mention of his name. 'He likes to tie six-pound weights to the feet before giving the upward

95

heave. Rather a nice touch, don't you think?'

Boysie hunched his shoulders at the thought.

'Just look behind you: to your left.'

Against the wall, he could make out a high, triangular shape.

'That is the rack, Mr Oakes: and I'm sure you know all about the rack.'

'Toast or clothes?' Again Boysie had surprised himself.

'Take him away,' said Sheriek, with genuine impatience. 'We will "resume play" – as I believe your cricket commentators say – after dinner. I cannot stand unpleasantness on an empty stomach. If you are not prepared to answer my question then, Mr Oakes ... well, we will see if the sight of Miss White on the *strappado* will help. Or maybe we will see how you like it. I think, Yacob, it might be an idea to bring the whips down as well. A few lashes on Miss White's shapely back could very well serve as an *hors d'oeuvre* to the entertainment. Meditate on these things, Mr Oakes. Meditate.'

Coral was lying on the bed when the Terrible Twins pushed Boysie back into the cellar.

'What's happened? Have you found out anything? Oh, your poor cheek – have they hurt you? What's going to happen to us?'

96

The questions tripped over one another.

'Let's have a cigarette first.'

He lit the filters and sat down beside her. She put her hand into his. There was no restraint between them. Strange how danger had brought them so close, thought Boysie. He felt he had known her for years – an immediate rapport had dispensed with any conventional period of adjustment.

'It was me they were after...' he started.

'You know, I don't even know your name,' said Coral, snuggling closer.

'My friends call me Boysie.'

'Boysie? Boy*sie*? *Boy*sie?' she repeated, trying it on for size. 'I like that.' Her face relaxed and she looked serious:

'Why have they got us here, Boysie? Please tell me.'

'There isn't a great deal to tell. If you must know... Well, the fact is... I sort of work for the Government – a glorified civil servant.'

'The Government! Golly, what a lark.'

'The thing is, those jokers want some information that just doesn't exist; and they're getting blasted unpleasant about it. Incidentally, there's another one besides the two cretins: some fellow with a slimy voice – sounded a bit of a queen to me: thought Boysie was an effeminate nickname.'

'I'm sorry,' she said, moving even closer. 'But, you know, I can't really take this seriously. Things like this just don't happen to people.'

'They do, and it's damn frightening.' Boysie thought he had said enough. It wouldn't do to tell her about the Bloody Tower next door: she'd find out soon enough. Burn Mostyn! Burn the Department; burn every burning thing. For a bewitched and suspended moment, he lapsed into the favourite silent pastime of railing on his boss.

'What are we going to do then?' The question had the disconsolate sound of a garden fete organiser defeated by a cloud burst.

'We can't escape from here: that's for sure. I suppose all we can do is sit tight and see what happens.'

'Oh.'

Coral, now upright on the bed, stretched out her legs: the compact body forming an elegant L – the attitude of a gymnast about to perform some drastic exercise. In this position, she contemplated her feet.

'Damn!' she said suddenly, licking her finger and applying it to a point low down on her left shin just below the bottom of her slacks.

'What's up?'

'Laddered my nylons. Blast.'

At a time like this, sighed Boysie. Women!

'Nylons in this weather?'

'Don't know why I put them on at all: it's too hot for stockings: 'specially under pants.

But we were going somewhere smart for lunch and She ... Daddy doesn't think a girl's properly dressed without nylons. I wore them as a sort of compromise, I suppose.'

Boysie had not noticed her near-slip with Sheriek's name. He looked down at his watch. The second hand made a complete revolution round the dial.

'Tell me the story of your life, Coral.'

'Me? Phooey! It would be much more interesting to hear about you.'

'The less you know about me the better.'

She had stopped doctoring the injured nylon.

'Seriously, Coral. What about you?'

'What about me? Oh, the usual: Cheltenham Ladies; RADA; no work; got mixed up with the beats, so Daddy brought me out here – to sit in the hot sun and cool off. Lucky really, he's quite flush.'

The conversation dwindled. Then she began again:

'What *are* they after?'

'They're after something which doesn't exist. They think I'm here on some hush-hush job...'

'And aren't you?'

'I'm here on holiday. On a harmless blistering holiday.'

'How boring.'

It would be better, thought Boysie, if there was some way of taking their minds off the

whole business. He slid his arm experimentally round her shoulder. The golden head
lolled close to his cheek and he again caught
the scent of lingering sunshine.

'They'll be coming back in about an hour:
to question me again.' He paused, wonder-
ing how much he should tell her. 'They
might bring you along as well. It could be a
bit rough – for both of us.'

'Don't fuss. We'll face that when it
happens.'

His hands were trembling:

'Got any ideas?'

'Such as?'

'Such as what we can do until then.'

She shifted, turning to face him:

'There's a rather old-fashioned recreation
for two that might suit,' she said, lying back
on the bed and tugging him gently towards
her.

For a girl who, outwardly, seemed so
naïve, Coral was most adroit. The little pink
tongue leaped out from between parted lips
as his mouth touched hers. Their bodies
pressed together, moulding belly to belly,
thigh to thigh; and almost immediately, her
breathing took on the rapid nasal heaviness
of passion.

'That was nice, Boysie. I liked that.'

'You're quite a girl,' said Boysie. He had
nearly forgotten the terror that lay behind
the door only a few feet away.

Coral slid off the bed and stood up:

'It always happens to me in the damnedest places,' she said, undoing the zip which snaked down the side of her sleek oyster silk pants.

The Sherkasiya – his favourite: a Circassian chicken delicacy served with a sauce of chopped nuts – had been excellent. Sheriek belched loudly. Gregory was a genius in the kitchen. He swilled out his mouth, swallowing the final half-glass of Pouilly Fuisse '56. Sheriek felt content.

The room was filled entirely with loot from the good old days – that never-to-return time when one could make a handsome living from the foolish and wealthy. He had been lucky then: always better at the sophisticated con game than this hectic cloak and dagger thing. Still, it was a living:

'Gregory,' he shouted. 'Coffee!'

The telephone began to ring as the brown gunman came into the room:

''Allo?' queried Sheriek into the antique-looking instrument.

'Is that Baudelaire?' The sound of his pass-name practically brought Sheriek to attention:

'It is "Ô Mort, vieux capitaine, il est temps! levons l'ancre,"' he quoted. 'Who wants me?'

'This is Chekhov. "If only we could go back to Moscow! Sell the house, finish with our life here, and go back to Moscow,"' the caller replied. Sheriek put his hand over the mouthpiece and beamed:

'Gregory! It is the Co-ordinator. The important one.'

'Can we talk?' asked the Co-ordinator.

'We are quite free.'

'Good. Have you carried out your instructions?'

'I have, Chekhov. And more besides. You will be very pleased. We have the Subject here – locked up.'

The pause was followed by a stinging spray of words – French, English, Russian and Italian. Most of them were obscene; all were highly insulting.

'But Chekhov... What is wrong?... I thought...' Sheriek was amazed. Finally, the abuse ended, and the Co-ordinator, calm again, spoke with chilling menace:

'What were your orders, my friend? I particularly wish to hear them from your own lips: because if anything goes wrong with this operation, I am going to hold you entirely responsible!' The last brace of words cracked like whiplashes.

'We have done wrong in apprehending this man?'

'You have probably only wrecked the whole plan. What were your instructions? What were you told?'

'We were given details of this Englishman–

"L". They said he was in the "highly dangerous" category. We were given his dossier and told that he would be arriving on the noon plane. We were to cover his arrival: identify him and check that he booked in at the Miramont in Menton. Later he was to be apprehended...'

'But you were to await orders?'

'Yes. But later he was to be apprehended – we had the opportunity...'

'Did your orders specifically say he was to be apprehended?'

'Not in so many words ... but I took it to mean...'

'Your orders in fact said that he would be taken care of in due course. Were you told whom you would be working under?'

'Oh, yes. You, Chekhov. They were very plain about that. We would be working under your absolute control.'

'Then can you tell me why you took it into your head to apprehend the Subject?'

Sheriek's voice quavered: 'I thought it would impress you of our integrity, Chekhov. We have many times been used as an assault group. I have just been interrogating this man...'

'You have not hurt him? If you have hurt one hair of his head, I will personally castrate you – with a blunt razor.'

'No, of course not.' Sheriek attempted to put a laugh into his hurrying voice. 'That comes later. We have simply been trying to find out why he is here...'

'But we know why he is here.'

'Oh.'

'He is on holiday.'

'That is what he told us... I didn't believe him ... I thought...'

'I am not interested in what you thought...'

'But, please, Chekhov... I believed it would help... I thought you would be pleased...'

'Now you listen to me,' the Co-ordinator cut into Sheriek's whine with the finality of a guillotine blade. 'For the first time in your paltry life, you have become involved in an operation of major international importance. You are out of your league, Baudelaire – that is a very apt American expression. This is one of the biggest things we have ever done. Its final implications would make your louse-ridden hair fall out – in handfuls. How many people have you in your cell?'

'My two usual men, and a girl – we have not used her before...'

'Is she safe?'

'She knows very little: simply in it for the money. I merely employed her as the come-on ... the bait.'

'She is not experienced then?'

'It depends which way you mean...'

'I mean operationally.'

'No, not really. No, she knows nothing.'

'In that case, I think you should drop her. Get rid of her – you understand me?'

'Yes, Chekhov. I understand.'

'And I want the Subject back in Menton within an hour. I don't care how you do it – you can even arrange an escape for him: but, if you do, for everybody's sake, make sure it looks authentic. He has seen your face, I suppose? He'd recognise you again?'

'No. No, I have been rather cunning there...'

'The others?'

'Yes, he has seen the others.'

'Keep them indoors until Monday night. As for you, I was going to use you simply as a local contact, but now?... I don't know. You had better be prepared to leave at a moment's notice – and I mean that: literally, a moment's notice. My own men will be doing any strong-arm stuff...'

'Yes, Chekhov. I'm sorry for my foolishness... I should have waited for your orders... But, really, I thought you would be pleased. It was a major triumph the way we lured him ... you should have seen my plan in action ... perfect ... timed to the last second ... if only Headquarters...'

'Shut up!'

'Yes, Chekhov.' The line was silent. 'Please ... may one ask how many of your cell are involved?'

'I have two men with me.'

'Thank you, Chekhov,' Sheriek fawned.

'Now, get the subject out of your house – At Speed!'

The line went dead.

The Co-ordinator, who went under the code-name Chekhov, tapped the glass-topped occasional table with long, delicate fingers and spoke softly:

'I shall have to arrange for a nasty accident. We must not have a buffoon like Sheriek making a mess of this one. It is much too big.'

Sheriek sat in silence. He was in despair. For him, this was the Moment of Truth. Sadly, he admitted that he was out of his depth with these people. For him, it was only a titillating game which he played with the flamboyance of a wealthy amateur. They were unadorned professionals, and it was a professional market. Sheriek mourned for the long-lost world. Things had changed. In an age of technocrats, he was a blunderer.

'Oh that I had stuck to honest stealing!' he said to nobody in particular.

'What is wrong, Excellency?' Gregory hovered with the coffee tray.

'Nothing that we cannot put right.' Sheriek had incredible powers of recovery, underlined with a buoyant optimism. 'Go and get Yacob and the girl. I must talk to all of you.'

'Yacob has gone down to the town, Excellency. We are nearly out of cognac, and I thought that if the Co-ordinator is coming…'

'Go and get the girl, then. We haven't much time.'

Coral came into the room, bright-eyed and somewhat dishevelled.

'He is a dish, isn't he, Sherry?'

'He looks a very frightened dish to me, my dear. But I'm afraid the ball is over. We must get him out of here – allow him to escape. There is no time to explain, but this means, Coral, my precious little parasite, that you will have to escape with him: help him.'

'In other words, Sherry darling, you've made a balls of it.'

'As you so charmingly put it, my dear, we have slightly overplayed our hand.'

'Well, I've tried everything I know. Best performance since my Juliet in Rep. Honestly, you should have heard me, Sherry – the Pony Club wasn't in it. By the way, he says he has nothing to tell you. Sorry, but really I did my best.'

'I'm sure you did – very beautifully too. The truth is, he has no information to give us.' He switched his eyes to Gregory: 'I want you to take the ignition key and put it in the car. Then find out if Yacob has returned – he must be briefed about the …. er … the impending "escape".'

When Gregory had left, Sheriek turned to the girl:

'I am sorry, Coral, my dear, but, for us, this must be the finish. Things are becoming, shall we say, warmish. I'm sorry.'

'The party's over? Oh well, there'll be other times and other places, Sherry. I'm sorry too, but... Well, that's show business.'

She took a cigarette from the heavy silver box on the table. Sheriek moved close and lit it for her. She saw that he was sweating; there were moist patches under his eyes and across his brow. But he meant nothing to her any more. It was over. In any case, he had only been a means to an end: a kick-provider. There were plenty more of those around. In her short life, Coral had bumped from many pillars and into a multitude of posts. To her, there was always something waiting just over the horizon. The future was ever rosy.

'You may keep the car, of course – you'll have to help him get away in it. It would be best, I think, if you got across the frontier as soon as possible. It would be safer.'

'Can I collect my things?'

'You have ten minutes to pack a case. Leave it in the hall and I will personally put it in the boot for you. Now, my dear Coral, before you go...'

He crossed to the tolerable El Greco

reproduction which hung above a genuine, ornate Desmalter jewel cabinet. The picture swung outwards from the wall, disclosing a circular safe.

'Just a small token of my appreciation, Coral,' said Sheriek.

For the second time in an hour, Coral unzipped her pants. But now it was to distribute the thick wad of mixed currency smoothly along the apricot tops of her nylon stockings.

Poor Coral: what a pity, thought Sheriek, eyeing the neat, flexible, half-clothed figure.

Between dwelling, happily, on his recent experience with Coral, Boysie had been passing the time by counting the bricks on the wall facing the bed.

Gregory followed the girl into the cellar – the ever-present Browning in his right hand, a cheap bottle of Côte de Provence and two glasses clasped dexterously in his left.

'What's this? Prisoner's last request?' said Boysie.

Coral made a shushing motion with her lips and Boysie leaned against the wall, silent until Gregory left the room.

'What gives?'

'I think there's some kind of panic on.' She poured the wine.

Boysie had a strange feeling that something was not quite as it should be. He took the glass from the girl's scarlet-tipped fingers, and sipped. The roughness of the drink made him cough and burned his stomach: he realised that, apart from picking at a small piece of cold chicken on the aircraft, he had not eaten since breakfast – and he had lost that at about 1500 feet over London. Yet something was out of place. He couldn't put his finger on it, but Gregory's departure from the cellar had not been normal.

'What happened?'

'Well, they took me upstairs... I've seen the other man by the way...'

'What's he like?'

'Fat. A bit of a smoothie. He asked me where I had met you, and how, and if I knew who you were. Then the telephone rang, and they took me into another room. After a bit, old Fatso came in and seemed to be all of a doo-dah. Said something about a conference. Seemed to be in a tremendous hurry: they couldn't get me back down here quick enough.'

'Wait a minute!' Boysie had caught on. Suddenly, he realised why Gregory's exit had seemed odd. He had not heard the locks pushed home on the other side of the door.

'What's up with you?'

'Hold your breath, cross your fingers and get out your prayer wheel. I think Camel-Face has made a bloomer.'

He went over and began to push his fingers into the crack between the door and its frame. The door swung towards them.

'Open Sesame!' breathed Boysie.

'The absolute, purblind, blithering idiot!' said Coral, still well in character. 'What are we waiting for?'

'It could be some kind of a trap.'

What a nervous bastard you are, she thought. Aloud, she said:

'Not it. I told you; they were in the hell of a panic.' She took a step towards the open door: 'Well, come on, Boysie: I'm getting out of here.'

'All right.' His throat felt parched in spite of the wine. The fear was returning:

'Keep close behind me.'

It was like standing on the high board at the school swimming pool. He took a deep breath, then, almost holding his nose, walked through the doorway and between the curtains.

Two strip-lights burned in the next room, revealing it to be a complete do-it-yourself torturers' workshop. Apart from the rack and pulley, a small electric furnace stood on a concrete plinth against the wall to their left. Beside the furnace, neatly arranged on a trestle table, lay a collection of interrogation tools: four cattle-branding irons, half a dozen sets of forceps, a box of bamboo spills, another of assorted pins and needles, three or four leather straps, a coil of rope, chains, and medical tray, set out with rubber gloves, tube and funnel. Boysie recalled how the medieval clergy had successfully exorcised unwilling devils by treating those possessed with a scalding holy water enema.

The mirror spots were set around a swivel chair at the far end of the mahogany table, behind which a short line of identically leather-backed books stood rigid on a low shelf. Leaning across the table, Boysie could read the titles: the complete works of the Marquis de Sade rubbed bindings with a translation of the *Ta T'sing Lu Li* – the code of the Manchu Dynasty which contained some honourable helpful hints on the problem of pain – and a couple of histories of the Inquisition.

The right end of the room was dominated by a dentist's chair and drill. Boysie's heart plummeted. Behind the chair, shut and solid, was a mammoth steel door.

'Try it,' prodded Coral.

The door was unlocked, giving way to a flight of stone steps leading up to an archway, curtained in claret velvet. Slowly they negotiated the stairway: edging up each step, hands flat against the rough plaster wall. At the top, Boysie squinted through the curtain. The hall was empty. A crouching brass cat held the front door ajar, and, from the awkward angle of the archway, he could just see the Continental, caught in a slash of light from the porch, its long opulent nose pointing to the right, away from the villa.

'The car's outside,' he whispered. 'If they've left the key...'

It would take them about thirty seconds, he reckoned, to get from the archway to the vehicle. He turned his head, concentrating on hearing any sound which might expose the presence of an ambush out of his line of vision. The house seemed still. Waiting.

'It's a straight run to the door.' He had leant back and put his mouth close to Coral's ear. 'There's a porch and some steps, I think – can't see it all. Make it as quickly and quietly as you can. OK?'

She nodded. Boysie turned his head and kissed her gently on the mouth: more to allay his own apprehension than to give her courage.

'Right? Go!'

They crossed the hall, Coral coming almost level with him as they reached the porch: their feet sounding hollow on the smooth tiles. Three broad steps led down to the drive: putting his foot on the bottom one, a bottle of brandy clutched loosely in his big right hand, was Yacob.

Returning from his errand, and still umprimed by Sheriek, Yacob let out a yell of alarm and raised the bottle.

At the Espionage School, Boysie had gained an Alpha Plus for both close combat and jujutsa: but never had he been called upon to put either of the arts into practice. Indeed, he had the direst doubts about their effectiveness outside the gymnasium – especially in his own hands and against a genuine assault. Frightened though he was, the past training set up an immediate body reflex. The action was completely automatic: all Boysie knew was the heart-flutter and stomach-leap as he came face to face with the huge Yacob.

He half-turned to the left and threw up his arm to parry the falling bottle. His right leg shot out and hooked behind Yacob's rising left knee. With a quick turn to the right, Boysie heaved back his leg and pushed forward with the whole weight of his body. Yacob opened his mouth as he felt his legs slide from under him. His arms flailed in an attempt to save himself, and he crashed, flat and heavy, down the steps, his head hitting the dry gravel with a juddering crunch.

Coral had reached the car and was tugging at the passenger door. She could see the key in the dashboard, but why wouldn't the door open? Sheriek had told her to make for the passenger door. She screamed at Boysie:

'The key's there, but I can't open the door.' Sheriek had said it had to be realistic, but the brush with Yacob had thrown her.

Boysie was down the steps and racing round to the driver's side. He pulled: the door shot open: half-in, half-out of the seat, he turned on the ignition, pressed the accelerator and stretched out to release Coral's door. The engine gave the steady growl of a successful start.

'Now!' said Sheriek quietly: standing next to Gregory in the doorway: 'Keep back, Yacob.'

The Browning banged twice – two seconds between each shot. Gregory had plenty of time to aim.

The first bullet caught Coral in the chest. She spun back against the car and then seemed to roll forward, staggering across the bonnet. The second bullet hit her in the neck. Boysie, frozen, one hand on the steering, the other on the doorhandle, saw the strange look of shock cross her face as she slithered down the front of the car, leaving a thick crimson smear on the white paintwork. He was holding his breath and could feel the back of his neck bristle like the hair on a dog at bay.

'Now to the left, Gregory – and, for God's sake, miss him,' said Sheriek.

The instinct of self-preservation was in Boysie. They were firing at him: he could hear the shots over the throb of the motor. He slammed the car into gear, released the brake and clutch in one movement and took off, zigzagging down the narrow drive. For a long time he had lived close to violence and sudden death, but here there was personal involvement. He had hardly known the girl and yet he had known her in the most complete sense. The warm, vital body he had held close only a short time ago, was now simply a useless lump of flesh, bones and organs – only the clothes on the cooling limbs still held any commercial value.

He wiped the film of vomit from his lips with the back of his hand, and flashed the lights full on. The drive ran, slightly down-hill, to a pair of ornamental iron gates, mercifully open. He stamped his foot on the brakes, then slewed the Continental out on to the road. Half a mile on, he saw the sign Beaulieu-sur-Mer. At least he was going in the right direction. A minute twister of mosquitoes, rising in the warm night air, hit the windshield, splattering themselves like great thunder-raindrops. Boysie's cold blue eyes concentrated on the winding road. Once more he had met with death, and this time his whole body and mind revolted against it. The old neuroses churned inside him all the way – through Monte Carlo and along the coast to Cap Martin.

As the road turned the headland, he could see Menton, slightly below and in front of him – a necklet of lights twinkling round the bay: the high white church floodlit, perched among a rising pack of houses in the old quarter.

Just before he reached the town, Boysie

swung the car into a side road and sat shivering and silent. It took him nearly ten minutes to regain control of his fractured nerves. All the time his mind banged out the same message: 'Iris mustn't see me like this: she mustn't know. Iris mustn't see me like this: she mustn't know...' And between each line, he saw the vivid, rapid, moving picture of Coral bumping down the side of the Continental: a corpse spread on the russet gravel.

At last he got out of the car and walked slowly towards the centre of the town. His legs were still shaking as he got to the Avenue Verdun.

Sheriek was sliding his hands up the stiffening thighs, removing the spread of bank-notes from behind the smooth, tightly-braced stocking-tops. His eyes were moist. Sheriek was an amateur.

At exactly 10.30 Boysie walked quickly through the foyer of the Hotel Miramont and took the lift up to the third floor.

5 – *CÔTE D'AZUR*

Saturday-Sunday June 8th-9th 1963

IRIS

'And about time too. I've been doing my nut...!' Iris opened the door – unsmiling, nose-high and eyebrows raised in the supercilious hauteur of a model-girl. Boysie pushed past her, closing the door and leaning back heavily on the frame:

'Lock it. Quick!'

'Oh God, Boysie, what's happened?' The cosmeticised mask, a disguise for her anxiety, crumbled when she saw his face: hair ruffled, a thin grime where sweat had dried, caked on his forehead and round his eyes; a long, livid graze – the work of Yacob's granite knuckles – running from right cheekbone to jaw.

'Boysie! Love! What the hell's happened?' Her arms were around him: her lips pressing his cheek. He clung to her for a moment: breathless and not a little flattered.

'I've been terrified, Boysie! I didn't know what to do. I even rang the hospital and asked them...'

Over her shoulder, he could see that she had been sitting in the armchair: a glass, still part-full, stood on the table:

'Lock the door. And get me a drink... Please sweetie.'

'OK. Sit down... Come on, sit down: you look terrible;' the distressed voice underlining her concern for him. She obeyed, turning the metal-tagged hotel key; and crossed to the trolley, landscaped with bottles, by the bathroom door:

'I rang down for something to drink, and they sent the lot ... and some Gauloises...'

'The ones I got went for a burton, I'm afraid...' Boysie was beginning to enjoy her solicitude.

'What are you going to have? Scotch?'

'A big, big Scotch. Dictator-size... Two fingers...' He held up his right hand, the middle and third fingers folded behind his thumb, index and little fingers stretched to their maximum spread of about five inches. She slopped the liquor into a tumbler, added two ice-cubes and brought it to him. He took a noisy gulp, spluttering as the ice banged against his upper lip, diverting some of the whisky: dribbling it from the corner of his mouth and down the chin. A thin stream of fire sank into his intestines, exploding like a minute Napalm bomb.

'Ah... Oi, Oi, Oi... That's better.' He was managing to put a curb on his wild breathing and the heart-bump had settled; then a small fresh wave of nausea bubbled into his throat, making him swallow hard.

Iris squeezed on to the chair, lighting a cigarette for him, and running the tips of her soothing fingers behind his neck.

'Ouch!' said Boysie, as she touched his lump.

'Sorry… Grief! What a bump, it's enormous. Shouldn't you see a doctor or something?' She was frowning, deep creases of concern etching up between symmetrical eyebrows: 'Can't you tell me what's happened, darling? Or is it the job – the Department?'

'In a minute, sweetie. Just let me get it sorted out. I've been coshed, doped, beaten up, threatened with torture and shot at – I feel like bloody Rip Kirby.'

'And you're bloody Boysie Oakes,' said Iris, gazing at the ridge of dried gore marking the area where the cosh had broken the skin behind his right ear.

Her legs were encased, snugly, in slate-grey tapering slacks, pinched tight at the waist, exaggerating the slim, curving overhang of her hips. The matching denim shirt, piped with white and monogrammed on the single pocket, was unbuttoned half-way down, giving Boysie a peek at the leafy, dark brassiere as she shifted closer. He put his hand on the slacks, high up on the inside of her thigh. Iris stiffened perceptibly; then, as though accepting the situation, relaxed.

'Bloody Boysie Oakes,' he mused. 'Honestly, I don't know ... I don't know what to do about this lot.' He had made several instinctive, and conflicting decisions on his way from the car to the hotel. In the long run, his only course of action was to get hold of Mostyn; and that, he reflected, was almost as dangerous as being at the unlikely mercy of big Yacob and the trigger-happy Gregory. But, there was nothing for it: he would have to take the risk:

'Look, I'll keep your name out of it, sweetie, but I really think I should ring Mostyn, I...'

'You can't.' She was nervous, like a timid wife trying to tell her muscular spouse-spanking mate that the housekeeping has all gone by Tuesday night.

'What do you mean, I can't?' Boysie had pushed forward and was sitting on the edge of the chair. From the look on her face, he detected an impending catastrophe.

'He rang... Just after you left, he rang here. He was on to us, Boysie. He knew I was with you, but anyway...'

'Oh my sainted, sacred aunt.' Boysie groaned and thumped his brow. 'That's bloody torn it that has... That's the blasted end...' The vision rose, luminous in his mind: the Court Martial; the Truth; all the deceits hustling into the open. They'd throw him to the lions! But Iris was still talking – quickly, as though anxious to get through:

'...No, Boysie, hang on a minute, it's not too bad... I think it's going to be all right... I mean he's not going to take it up to the Chief or anything like that. The point is ... well, there's a job for you... You're... You're OPERATIONAL.'

'*Oh, no!*'

'Oh, yes. He said to tell you: "Pressure". Does that mean anything? I hadn't heard it before.'

It meant a whole lot. Since quarter-to-five that afternoon, Boysie had been subjected to a battery of shocks. But the one innocuous word, 'Pressure', spoken by a man sitting behind a heavy, opulent desk in Whitehall, was the big pay-off: the knock-out blow, swinging up from the canvas to lift him off his feet. 'Pressure' was his personal code alert: the warning that a 'kill' was imminent.

Even at moments of lowest physical and mental ebb, Boysie had never dared think of a situation like this. To be ordered in to the kill at this particular juncture, and in this particular place, was disastrous. The circumstances were of the stuff from which nightmares were made. A kill when he was away from home: cut off: vulnerable: out of touch with...

It didn't bear thinking about, and the first

hysterical movements of panic began to come screaming out of their holes deep in the heart of his mind. He forced them back, clinging to the slender hope that, still, something might save him from yet another death.

'Is that all he said? All Mostyn said? Haven't we got to go back to London or anything?' He was floundering for words: for an excuse: for escape.

'No. I think, in a way, he was glad you were out when he telephoned. He doesn't want any personal contact with you. Said that was *very* important.'

It was getting worse. A great thunder-cloud, heavy with depression and danger, had swept up, covering the whole limit of his lonely horizon. In the over-used words of the proverb, this was out of the blasted skillet and on to the gas ring.

'He didn't even hint at...' In time he stopped short at the word 'Target'. Iris knew a whole hatful of secrets; but he was pretty sure that she had no inkling of his own ghoulish position in the organisation. She was speaking again.

'...a courier is arriving ... here, tomorrow... With all the information for you. You've got to stay in the hotel and I'm to pick him up in Nice. At noon...'

Inserting two fingers into the shirt pocket, she drew out a sheet of embossed hotel notepaper folded into a sharp oblong. Boysie took it from her, opened it and looked down at the round, girlish capital letters:

KIDAGLG: MYLHWLAG. WRKDU-ANGNDA: KDWDARG. WRBFDABR: RWTNAR, he read. That damn code, he thought. I'll be up half the night trying to make sense of it. Iris was still pattering out her instructions:

'I've got to wait in the main lounge at the airport – noon – the courier will know me and contact. Are you all right, Boysie?'

Boysie was not all right. With his eyes closed, he was allowing his addled brain to do some advanced research into the myriad things that could go wrong:

'Another drink,' he muttered like a man coming out of an anaesthetic.

'All right, love.' She laughed. 'Poor old Boysie; gets a job of work just when he wants to play. Don't look so worried. It's probably nothing very big.'

Boysie woke up to the fact that he was making a fool of himself in front of the girl: that his inversion and desperate attitude must appear to her as an emotional over-dramatised act. Whatever else (even if he had to stay awake all night to ward off the horrors which might set him rambling loudly in his sleep), he mustn't give the game away: she was far too close to Mostyn.

He opened his eyes and leaned back in the chair, willing himself into normality.

'That's right.' His voice calmer now that he had faced the situation. 'Laugh at me.'

Iris was pouring another large Scotch and mixing a gin and tonic for herself. She giggled:

'Sorry, Boysie, but you looked like the ad on telly. You know: "I do wish he would relax. He's so tense."' Then, serious: 'I say? Do you think this has anything to do with what happened to you tonight?'

'Could be.' It was highly possible. 'The burkes who clobbered me were certainly tourists.' He used the general slang for opposition agents.

Iris put the replenished glass into his hand.

'You say the courier will make contact with *you?*' asked Boysie.

'Colonel Mostyn said he would know me. After all, I suppose I know far more of the boys – by sight, anyway – than you do.'

Boysie's stomach, reacting to the large doses of whisky, gave a low, undignified rumble. In spite of his preoccupation with the forthcoming kill, and its attendant tensions, he realised that he was very hungry.

'Have you eaten yet?' He looked up at her: gastric juices running at the thought of vast menus written large in scrolled, Gothic, incomprehensible French.

'No ... I ... I was waiting for you. I'd almost forgotten about food.'

'Hungry now?'

She nodded.

'We'd better have something sent up.'

He pulled her on to the chair, then realised, from the sluggishness of his bodily reactions, that he had already taken the edge off his sexual appetite earlier that evening. The ghost of Coral White passed across the room.

'Hey! Penny for them?' Iris had her mouth half open: waiting to be kissed. He planted a quick peck on the end of her nose and stood up, lifting her with him:

'Grub,' said Boysie.

The events of the last few hours, particularly the most recent disturbing news, had turned his thoughts from the obsessive and inordinate desire for Iris. Now, as he stood close to her, the erotic fantasies stirred once more. Through their clothes, he could feel her young belly, soft as spring moss, moulding to his. Then, with mild dismay, he realised that, at this precise moment, he couldn't have satisfied a quick-action nymphet let alone the luxurious Iris. His enthusiastic tumble with the dear departed Coral had near-sterilised him. The dead blonde haunted him again.

Boysie's grasshopper mind – always most active when his pride was affected –

jumped, from the necrophiliac thoughts, back to the kill round the corner. It was no good getting steamed up about that either, he thought. Whatever else happened, he would not get positive target identification, or location, until tomorrow afternoon. After that there might still be a chance: still time for him to make the usual arrangements: to go through the ritual he always followed after a 'Pressure' signal arrived. In the meantime? Well, he'd have to see about that … after they had eaten. One good thing about it – he counselled himself, walking to the telephone – I'll be much safer staying in here with the door locked. Yacob and Gregory might still be on the prowl.

'I'll ring down for a menu. Got to keep your strength up, you know.'

Iris winced. It was the remark of an almost passé wolf trying to convince himself.

'That's more like my Boysie,' she said silkily.

Half-an-hour later, with Boysie washed, brushed up and a little less numb, they dined. The warm night air rustled the curtains and shook the candle flames. The candles had been the waiter's idea, and the whole affair was produced with a profes- sional romantic care resembling Hollywood in its glossy, goo period. Even the snow- coated servant performed his duties as if they were part of some exotic, complicated love-play. All that's missing, thought Iris, is the gypsy violinist. Boysie remarked:

'You simply couldn't get service like this, at this time of night, anywhere in London. You just couldn't get it.'

The scampi was fresh and tender (as Boysie said: 'None of your old pre-packed deep freeze stuff here'): the *Sauce Tartare* perfect, with an explicit blending of the tarragon, capers, gherkin and shallot: its bite accenting the full flavour of the prawns. At the arrival of the silver dish of *Cote de veau Foyot* – the veal nestling on a mound of sweet green peas – Boysie began to exploit his parroted culinary knowledge: giving Iris a stir by stir account of how the cutlets were rolled in Parmisan, then baked in a stock of white wine, fried onions and butter.

When the percolator was popping regularly on the spirit lamp, and the iced melon – stuffed with raspberries marinaded in Kirsch – had been served, the obsequious waiter retired. Boysie, well mellowed by the whisky, and an insipid Couhins Rose, gave Iris a racy, highly-ornamented and, at times, expurgated version of the kidnapping incident. He omitted the last five minutes of horror outside the villa – blocking it from his mind with the excuse that he did not wish to upset the girl. The conversation flagged, picked up again and finally, with the third cup of coffee, petered out. It was one o'clock before Iris made the first move and suggested that it was time for bed.

The waiter returned to clear the remnants while Boysie performed his nightly toilet, emerging from the bathroom to find Iris waiting to take his place, loaded with feminine equipment:

'Won't be long, darling. Just going to have a quick bath.' She looked him up and down. 'Get you!' she said, and, with a flap of the wrist, was inside, with the door closed, before he could reply.

Boysie threw his recently discarded clothes on to the chair and looked at himself in the full-length mirror which formed the door to the built-in wardrobe. It was the black lounging jacket that did it, he decided, stroking the sharkskin lapels. It went well over the midnight-blue and gold silk pyjamas, but one had to admit that the whole effect was a bit much. He turned slowly, studying himself from all angles, noting that the jacket was being pulled out of place by the weight of the gun in the right pocket. He went to the bedside table and opened the drawer. Taking out the pistol, he slid back the breech, cocking the weapon. He thumbed the safety-catch on to 'safe' and dropped the gun into the drawer, closed it and returned his attention to folding and tidying the clothes. He was about to drape the slacks over a hanger when he remembered Mostyn's message. The paper was there, in his hip pocket, crumpled but intact. Boysie took it to the writing table, angled in the corner opposite the bed, spread it on the blotter, and switched on the shaded lamp. The line of letters stared back at him, an inexplicable jumble:

KDAGLKG: MYLHWLAG. WRKDU-ANGNDA: KDWDARG. WRBFDABR: RWCNAR.

He looked at his watch. 1.25. Sunday morning. Right. He sat down, took a small sheaf of notepaper from the leather container, and picked a pencil from the rack. Closing his eyes, Boysie groped round his memory for the Sunday Sentence. On Sundays it was *Romeo and Juliet.*

Boysie's personal code was based upon the famous Max Klausen cipher – virtually unbreakable unless one is supplied with the key sentence. From the beginning, Boysie had been provided with a sentence for each day of the week: all from Shakespeare. Hence, Monday was a passage from *Coriolanus,* Tuesday, it was the *Taming of the Shrew,* Wednesday, *Othello* – right up to *Hamlet* on Saturday and *Romeo and Juliet* on Sunday. As he rarely had to use the code, the whole business often seemed rather childish; and the decoding operation, when it had to be done, invariably took on the

131

chalky atmosphere of prep in the Lower Third: an arduous, irksome chore. Laboriously he wrote his Sunday Sentence in large capitals – a segment from Mercutio's Queen Mab speech: 'Her chariot is an empty hazel nut, Made by the joiner squirrel or old grub, Time out o' mind the fairies' coachmakers.' Then, following the memorised pattern, he inserted the letters of the alphabet until the key was complete:

HER CHARIOT IS AN EMPTY
a b c d   e   f g h   i   j   k l   m

  HAZEL NUT,
    n   o   p

MADE BY THE JOINER SQUIRREL
q   r   s   t

OR OLD GRUB, TIME OUT O' MIND
    u

THE FAIRIES' COACHMAKERS
  v   w   xyz

Boysie lit a short panatella from the box he had ordered with the dinner, and began to decode the message. The first two words came out:

WQEUOWU: KMOA-OEU

'Oh, hell!' said Boysie, with feeling. 'It

always happens to me. There's been a cock-up somewhere.' He got up and hammered on the bathroom door:

'Iris!'

'You can't come in. Go away.'

'I don't want to come in. It's about this bloody message: are you sure you got it right?'

'Of course I did.' A note of alarm: 'Why?'

'I've started to decode it, and it's coming out like an optician's test card.'

'Boysie, I'm certain I got it right.'

'Well, I don't know what's up. You haven't been pulling my leg, have you? He did send this?' Perhaps it was Mostyn up to some trick.

'Don't be an idiot. I took it down over the telephone – just after you left.'

'Just after…?' Boysie was deflated. 'It's all right. It's okay. I see where we've gone wrong.' The message had been passed to Iris early on Saturday evening. He had been using his Sunday sentence.

'As a secret agent,' he muttered to himself, once more in the mirror, 'you'd make a damn good lavatory attendant.' He chuckled to himself, thinking of the tag-line: 'I could take holidays at my own convenience.' Then, in the voice of a TV man doing a hard sell, he added: 'Saturday is *Hamlet* day.'

Once more he set to work. His *Hamlet* text was part of the melancholy Dane's irate

133

comment to his Mum, Gertrude. 'Just after' – as Mostyn had once drawled – 'old man Polonius got a rapier through his arras.' Now, the final result read:

LOOK HERE UPON THIS PICTURE;
a b   c d   e f g h   i j   k l m

AND
n   o

ON THIS; THE COUNTERFEIT
                                p

PRESENTMENT
          q

OF TWO BROTHERS. SEE WHAT A
    r   s

GRACE

WAS SEATED ON THIS BROW;

HYPERION'S
u

CURLS; THE FRONT OF JOVE
                          v   w
HIMSELF
          xyz

Fifteen minutes later, he had the full translation:

KDAGLKG: MYLHWLAG. WRKDU-ANGNDA: KDWDARG. WRBFDABR: RWCNAR now read: CONTACT: QUADRANT. RECOGNITION: CORONET. RESPONSE: ERMINE.

Boysie memorised the facts. The contact's code reference was 'Quadrant'; the operational identification, 'Coronet', and the reply identification, 'Ermine'. He wondered what sardonic double-entendre was contained in the words 'Coronet' and 'Ermine'. Mostyn usually thought of some bizarre twist when allocating operational codes. A project which had covered the disposal of a homosexual rocket expert, recently in Manchester, had been labelled 'Guided'; with the response 'Muscle'.

Coronet and Ermine? Wouldn't be surprised if he wanted me to knock off the flaming Duke of Edinburgh, thought Boysie as he started to tear the little pile of papers into small pieces prior to burning them. By the time he had finished, Iris's quick bath had taken exactly fifty-five minutes. He yawned. The opiate effect of the alcohol was wearing off: the throbbing returning to his head, and a dull rheumatic ache settling into his joints. Fatigue was beginning to drown him; and, any minute now, Iris would appear, ready for the consummation: the sole purpose of their clandestine weekend.

Boysie swore obscenely to himself. This was the climax to months of hard preparation; and now he had to admit that he felt about as much like it as a eunuch on the day shift.

But, to some measure, he had reckoned without Iris. She came out of the bathroom looking, he imagined, like a bride on her wedding night: which, to be quite fair, had been her intention.

The burnished copper hair, released from its elegant upsweep, was tied with a single ribbon behind her neck. A double-layer of lime nylon fussed in a waterfall of frills round her throat and over her breasts, dropped loosely to the waist, then flounced to a provocative point below the knees. Through the opaque texture of the material, Boysie could half-see the pink, fresh line of her naked body.

'Not in bed yet?' She did not look at him, her eyes resting on a point six inches in front of Boysie's feet.

'Whenever you say.'

Between the sheets, with the light out and silence folding them like a heavy velvet curtain, Boysie reached out for her, his hand slipping behind her shoulders, their mouths searching for one another in the darkness. Her tongue found his, fencing and probing.

Boysie battled with exhaustion, reacting to every move, vainly and without the complete abandonment and expertise which had flavoured his dreams. It was Iris who took the initiative, her hands fumbling with his pyjamas and sliding her nightdress high over her waist.

Boysie was amazed to find how prepared she was: agile, supple, responding to each flexing move. They made love in silence, except for a low moan from Iris, between their limpet mouths, at her ultimate moment – reached, to Boysie's lasting chagrin, many minutes before he could complete the act. The long-awaited time had come and gone – an undoubted anti-climax, with Boysie near to humiliation.

At last Iris fell asleep. Quietly disentangling himself, Boysie turned over and allowed consciousness to sink away. Then, with a falling jerk, he was awake, the sight of Coral's violent last seconds penetrating to the surface of his mind. He began to think about death and the possibility of a future existence. His stream of thoughts meandered into the region of his job and he considered the twenty-five corpses, marked to his credit since he had been pressed into service. His conscience leaped in, questioning with logical morality. Death. Death. Death. Then the real facts began to take shape, old fears whispering in his ear.

'Oh, my God,' he murmured into the pillow. 'How ever did I get involved in this?' And Boysie Oakes, Liquidator for the Department of Special Security, thought about Truth and the jungle of deception he had grown and twisted round himself.

6 – *CÔTE D'AZUR*

Sunday June 9th 1963

'L' –

All hope of sleep had gone. When Boysie's anxious neuroses started to play him up in the middle of the night, it was like being plagued by raging mental toothache. Stretched among the rumpled bed-clothes, with the gorgeous Iris reduced to the common denominator of a snore, Boysie allowed his brain to toss around, stormily sifting through the past. He put out his hand, feeling for the cigarettes and lighter.

The spurt of flame made him screw up his eyes, until the cigarette was burning and the taste of cool smoke tickled the back of his throat. The flame left a sheet of colour dancing in his vision: a pool of red, turning to yellow and finally into sparkles of light studding the darkness. Gradually they diminished until sight returned to normal, and, through the gloom, he could make out the oblong window, the mirror and part of the chair.

Iris had joked about his use of filter-tips.

'They're cheats,' she had said. It was true enough, he supposed. This was an outward sign of his uneasy love-hate-fear relationship with mortality. He began to wonder about the moment of death – the final drifting from familiar life into the unknowing of infinite sleep. As a boy, he had been certain that things would never change: sure that he was the big exception: the one who would never reach the grave. He used to look out of the cottage windows, up to the soft edge of the downs, and imagine that there was no such thing as decay. Remembering that time, his childhood seemed to have been one of everlasting sunshine – thirty, thirty-five years ago. Now, with his shoulder to forty-five, he felt that death was hanging round him like some outlandish aura.

This morbid obsession was a recent facet of Boysie's continual nervousness: stemming, he imagined, from the elephantine sense of guilt: from his big deception. There had been a time – his first years with the Department – when he was able to treat the thing as a huge joke. But, of late, there were moments when the giggle had turned sour.

How did it all begin? Where did it start? What was it that made him behave as he did? Was it Paris? Certainly there was no hint before that August afternoon, among the sweltering rues and avenues and boulevards, the torn Nazi posters and the faded

Dubo-Dubon-Dubonnet advertisements. Even after the Paris thing, life had been normal: he used to think about the incident, yet he was never haunted by fears.

These anxieties had certainly not started before Paris. Nothing could have been more prosaic than his childhood when – against a backdrop of downs, woods and good growing soil – he had progressed from village school to a scholarship at the local grammar: a likeable lad unhindered by bad dreams and fantasies. True, he could remember that, as a very small boy, he had hated to see cruelty or death meted out to any living creature. He had cried over the stiff, untwittering bodies of birds, had hysterics when his mother drowned a litter of kittens, and suffered agonies of remorse after accidentally squashing a beetle.

All tiny, living things – even the dreaded spiders – were safe when the infant Boysie was around. But there was nothing abnormal about that – nothing 'screwy' as his old Ma would say. He fought, played, swore, took a pride in being fit, and got up to all the filthy tricks of boyhood. When, at last, the time came for him to be foisted on to an ambushed world – armed with a mediocre school certificate – he chose the safest of dull desk jobs: in the rating department of the borough council offices in a nearby market town.

Among the woolly headed typists, Boysie discovered the joys of being a man. Healthy, muscular, with an overt love of his own body, he was soon invested with a reputation for being a bit of a 'lad' with the girls. Indeed, in those quiet, tractor-humming last country days of peace, the quest for ripe maidens became, virtually, a hobby. He was in good company, for, by village tradition, this was the pastime for most of the growing boys: and, to be honest, the girls liked nothing better – in the spring and summer – than to lie on their backs, basking in long, straw-strewn sessions behind the hay-ricks, barns and copses: their wild, weekend trysting places.

When the war came, Boysie – like most of his friends – marched off to do battle. The girls sobbed a little, and Sunday-walked to their favourite dells, and sighed. They had no way of knowing that, in a few years, their needs would be amply satisfied by the big, well-set-up, nasal men from across the Atlantic. But Boysie was now a soldier – though it is doubtful if his mind ever touched on the realities of death, courage, blood or mutilation. The war, to him, was really only an extension of the bang-bang games of cowboys and Indians, or British and German (World War I vintage) – where the dead got up at the end of the day and toddled home to tea.

As it happened, Boysie never saw action throughout the whole of his Service career. By some stroke of incredible executive genius, his name seemed to have been placed on a list earmarked for continual courses, transfers and postings. No sooner had he finished an advanced weapon training course, than he found himself whipped off to join a newly formed unit. From there, he was promptly sent on a signals course, which he failed, necessitating a posting back to the weapon training course. So it went on, right up to the day he reported to an armoured regiment – on an NCOs' course for tank commanders. The reason for this last extraordinary change in his circumstances was entirely due – though he never knew it – to the fact that a randy orderly room corporal had, at a crucial moment, tickled the breasts of a scrawny ATS filing clerk: distracting the girl, and causing Boysie's file to be dropped into the wrong box.

Boysie never complained about his treatment. He even enjoyed the varied life – five weapon training courses, transfers to three different regiments, a signals course (failed), three heavy weapons courses, a catering course (abandoned), a transport course and the tank commanders' course. There was little responsibility, and life in the training camps, haunted by him between 1939 and 1944, had a sense of chaotic order which he appreciated. One usually had a pretty good idea of what was going to happen next. Moreover, there were whole platoons of nubile ATS girls, always ready and willing to drop their service issue (khaki: rayon) at the twitch of a battle-dress trouser leg.

Even on the firing ranges – thumping away with rifles, brens, stens and revolvers – Boysie seldom reflected on the ultimate use of these lethal pieces of equipment. For him, shooting was exciting only in so far as it gave him the opportunity to prove his fine standard of co-ordination between eye and muscles.

So, he was shuttled around, fed, clothed, satisfied and regularly paid. The war was good, and inoffensive, to Boysie. That is, until the hot August day in Paris when he first collided with that irrevocable responsibility which is involved in the business of killing. And the whole of the Paris thing was really a chapter of dreadful accidents.

On the day in question, Sergeant Boysie Oakes, complete with tank and crew, was hopelessly lost. They had been in France for barely two days – making the journey rapidly from the coast to arrive only a few hours after fighting ceased, and the main force had liberated the joyous city.

First, the radio packed up. Then, already bewildered by a veritable guide-book of orders, map references and countermanded instructions, they lost contact with the remainder of the troop. Somewhere near the Madeleine, Boysie – concentrating on Paris and not on his job – ordered the driver to turn left instead of right. Within a couple of minutes, they had ploughed into a peeling, flustering jungle of back streets. Boysie, anxious to prove that he was in complete command of the situation, issued a series of instinctive, authoritative-sounding orders: relying solely on his non-existent sense of direction to bring them back under the safe shelter of the Troop Commander's wing. Instead, they began to travel in an ever-increasing circle. For the best part of an hour, they rumbled aimlessly around Paris, and, for all that could be seen of other Allied forces, they might well have been the only detachment engaged in shifting Hitler's jack-booted heel from the soil of France.

It was diabolically hot, and, though Boysie's comrades-in-arms were not a particularly bright bunch, they soon fastened on to the fact that their leader was not only out of his depth but also clasping at imaginary straws. They began by muttering among themselves, and shouting occasional words of abuse up through the turret hatch where Boysie, grinning sickly at the occasional waving Parisian, wrestled with maps and compass.

Finally, the driver pulled over to the side

of the road, stopped their clanking sun-trap, and announced that – court martial or no – he wasn't going any farther until bleeding Sergeant Oakes had got down from the ditto tank, discovered where they ditto were, and worked out a ditto good route which would reunite them with their ditto friends.

The street seemed horribly deserted, but Boysie, with no alternative, climbed down and began to amble along the pavement. It was at this point, that he glanced down a narrow side street and saw the three struggling men. Hesitating, he started towards them. Then it happened, with the jerky speed of an old silent film: one of the men – with his back to the wall, taking most of the punishment – was shouting at him:

'Help! Quickly! I'm British! Help! Intelligence!'

The other two looked up, saw Boysie, and started to run. He couldn't possibly catch them on foot so, intending simply to fire a warning shot into the air above their heads, Boysie pulled at the stud-fastening on his webbing and lugged the heavy Colt .45 out of its holster: lifting it, to aim high between the tall buildings.

Usually, Boysie was exceptionally careful about things like safety catches. But, on this occasion, as he admitted to himself later, the catch must have already been set to 'fire' when the gun was bedded down in his holster. As the Colt came level with his waist, he automatically moved his thumb, to release the catch from the 'safe' position. It didn't budge and the increased pressure caused his finger to tighten on the trigger. He felt the jerk, and almost jumped out of his boots at the explosion, magnified in the constricted alleyway. The thing had gone off in his hand. Worse still, the shock set up a reflex, and before he could stop himself, the trigger-finger squeezed back a second time.

It was not until Boysie reached the men that he realised, through a sadistic trick of fate, both bullets had been deadly accurate. Mostyn never knew that only a pure fluke had saved him, instead of his assailants, from being carved up by one of the two chunks of spinning lead.

Boysie, incredulous at the sight, skidded to a halt, his heavy boots sounding like a well-shod horse's hooves on the rough cobbles. From the bright sunlight he had come into this harmless little street and shot two men. In less than half a minute he had stopped two hearts, cut off the vocal chords in two throats, and bunged up a couple of pairs of ears and eyes. He opened his mouth to say something about it being a terrible accident, but the words would not come. The tousled man, panting against the wall, was muttering his thanks and talking about it being a 'damned good show'. But Boysie just stood, planted into the ground, immobile and appalled.

He could feel the muscle control going at the corners of his mouth, the left side curving upwards, more than usual – as it always did when he was nervous or under any kind of pressure. His eyes, fixed in shock, seemed to be tied, in revolting fascination, to the two dead things at his feet. This was the strange look of terror, incredulity, agitation and emotion which Mostyn saw and translated into terms of psychopathic bloodlust.

Boysie was so dazed that he took Mostyn completely on trust. The Major – as he was then – explained the situation: how the two dead men were Nazi undercover boys and he was with British Intelligence – and a pack of other stuff which Boysie neither understood nor bothered to take in. Mostyn took Boysie's name, rank and number, said that he might be called upon to make a statement, and returned with him to the tank, which, by this time, had been joined by a scout car – searching for them with a come-home-all-is-forgiven message from the fatherly Troop Commander.

Boysie heard no more about the incident, though the swift finality of its violence stayed with him for many years. Eventually, he reconciled himself with the thought that he had only done his duty: the men were enemies. Admittedly the circumstances were odd, but if ordered into action his scoreboard of killings would have been considerably higher.

Climbing down from the tank, following a routine inspection three days after the shootings, Boysie's boot slipped on the metal and he crashed on to a hard French road, breaking three ribs and both legs. Within the week he was propped up in a military hospital near Oxford, encased in plaster and being coddled by a raven-haired nurse whom he later seduced on a still evening in Christchurch Meadows.

It was in hospital that Boysie met Philip Redfern – a Catering Corps sergeant from Kettering – suffering, at that time, from a serious burn caused by scalding fat: a wound received, late and unsteady, one night in the Sergeants' Mess kitchens. They took to each other at once, and when they were well enough to go out on little convalescent sprees, they went together. Indeed, both were after that same nurse; Boysie winning by a tea, and pictures at the Electra.

Neither had any fully developed plans for dealing with the imminent dangers of peace (Boysie having no desire to return to the bosom of his village-bound family); so it was natural that, in time, they decided to join up in an unspecified venture which, as they assured each other, would eventually make their fortunes.

After one or two false starts – during which they lost their generous gratuities, and Redfern acquired Mona, a busty ex-barmaid, as his wife – the two rather unenterprising partners set themselves up in the Bird Sanctuary Café and Aviary.

For five years they thrived. Then, in the winter of 1953, Boysie – who left most of the finance to the Redferns – discovered that Mona's growing and unquenchable thirst, had quaffed a large percentage of the profits. They were well and truly in the bright crimson; and there was a row, of sorts, ending in a general resolution to pull in their horns.

Until then they had seemed to be riding high: now, business began to drop off, and the expensive collection of feathered friends in the aviary started to moult. Money was a perpetual headache and the bank manager stopped calling them 'sir'.

By 1955 Mona had lost all interest in the café, and most of her self-respect. Her alcoholic capacity was diminishing as rapidly as her reputation, and she was becoming not only an embarrassment to her husband and Boysie, but also a general liability to the business. Even so her death, in a blazing car after a hectic three-day bender, came as a dreadful shock. Redfern lost heart, Boysie became anxious and the Bird Sanctuary Café and Aviary slipped into their final phase of its sear and yellow age.

A year later, when Redfern had his accident and died, Boysie was left carrying the complete can. The mortgage had not been paid for three months and the Building Society was threatening to foreclose. The bank still moaned. A few days after they buried Redfern, Boysie had a lengthy, and uncomfortable, session with the accountant. Debts amounted to £4,262 10s 4d, and he decided that the only thing possible was to cut his losses, get out and try for a new start. He was then thirty-eight years old; trained for nothing in particular, moderately intelligent and with no true roots. He had four local girl friends, whom he visited in strict rotation; a dozen or so acquaintances; and no overpowering ambitions. If he managed to get a fair price for the business, and was able to pay all the debts, he could reckon on being at financial zero – neither owing nor solvent.

As Boysie stood at these cross-roads of life, pondering the possibilities of emigration, the past and future merged in the visiting personage of James George Mostyn. If he had planned it, Mostyn could not have chosen a better psychological moment.

Iris was away, deep in dreams of handsome young men, golden sands and slinky dresses. Boysie looked at her, envious of the complete inertia. He lit another cigarette and slipped from between the sheets, feeling his way to the chair. Putting on his lounging jacket, he went over to the balcony window; then, remembering the possible presence of Yacob or Gregory, drew back: returning to the chair, his mind scrambling about, trying to fix some definite blame on to Mostyn. The blasted man had never given him a chance: the operation, which took him out of the old life and into the new, had been so smooth; so calculated – and the money had been so good.

This exercise of memory, in the wee small hours, brought back a dozen ghosts: his own unsubstantial figure appearing among them as the least real – a shadow; an ectoplasmic jotting in the margin of events. If Boysie of the pre-Mostyn days had walked through the door at this moment, he thought, it would be impossible to recognise him – a different man, from another world: from a land untouched by Mostyn's satin manner, 'withit' philosophy, arty undercurrent and sharply defined system of values: a person who might never have existed.

The Bird Sanctuary Café and Aviary seemed a hundred years away; and when he thought of Mostyn's sudden intrusion, there was that same sense of shock, experienced when the second-in-command had first revealed the enormity of his mission.

The Bentley had pulled up in front of the café a little before midday. Boysie, going over a pile of bills in the office, heard the door open and footsteps cross to the snack-bar. He got up and went through to find Mostyn, grey-suited, looking a little older, lounging over the counter:

'Remember me, Sergeant Oakes?' The voice had an edgy drawl: the voice of a man who wanted something, and was pretty sure of getting it. Boysie wondered if it was going to be a spot of blackmail. He had recognised Mostyn at once – his body flushing warm, a physical memory of the killings.

'Blow me!... Major?... Wait a minute, it was in Paris ... I remember .. Major?'

'Mostyn, old son... Colonel now... Colonel Mostyn.'

Boysie had an uneasy feeling that the little rat eyes held a slight glitter of contempt:

'Well, fancy seeing you, sir...' Inside himself, he recalled the man leaning against the wall regaining breath while the shots still numbed his eardrums:

'Can I get you anything? Something to eat? Meal perhaps?'

'No, thank you, Sergeant Oakes. Or can I call you Boysie?'

Now he was really on guard:

'How did you know that? Boysie, I mean?'

'Ah,' said Mostyn cryptically, 'how

indeed? Just thought I'd look you up. Heard you were here, you know. Couldn't pass without saying hallo. Can't pass a bloke who's saved your life.'

Boysie didn't like this one bit: there was a sense of thunder in the air:

'No, I suppose not. You sure I can't get you something. Cup o'tea?'

'Been a long time,' said Mostyn, ignoring the hospitality.

'Yes.' Boysie did not sound at all keen. 'Yes, quite a long time.'

Mostyn raised his eyes and looked round the café, his face impassive. For the first time, Boysie noticed what a seedy place it had become: the wallpaper drab; paint flaking from the window frames; the tables, solid and stained with their grubby linen and cheap, plastic sugar holders. There were stale crumbs on the counter, and a damp patch, marked with a sugary-brown ring, where someone had placed a wet, unsaucered cup. 'Anybody else around, old Boysie?'

'Anybody else? Why, sir? I mean…?'

'I want to talk to you, old Oakes. It's rather…' he inspected his aseptic fingernails '…important.'

Boysie found himself wishing for a charabanc of tea-thirsty trippers:

'The cook's out the back and the waitress will be here any time. I suppose we'd better go into the office.' He indicated the way through the door which led to the living quarters, adding an unenthusiastic: 'If it's important.'

'You have a waitress too? My, my!' Iced treacle.

Mostyn followed him behind the counter, pausing to try for dust on one of the tables. He looked at his fingers and pulled a distasteful face:

'Have to give your waitress a rocket. Not doing so well, eh?'

'Can't grumble.' Boysie was not giving anything away. By now he had made up his mind that Mostyn was out of the service and working for some blasted financial recovery firm. They faced each other in the small untidy room.

'Bit of a shock, your partner's death?' said Mostyn, removing a pile of papers – held between finger and thumb – from the spare chair.

'You know about that? Terrible. I'm still a bit... Well, all to pieces, if you know what I mean?'

Oh dear, thought Mostyn, we shall have to do something about that accent; and the clothes – the Harris Tweed jacket must be all of five years old. Ugh! Aloud, he said:

'I can imagine. Still, death's no stranger to you, is it, old boy?'

'Oh, I don't know.' Nonplussed.

'The two men in Paris. Remember? And

there must have been others, old Oakes, there must have been others.'

'The men in Paris. Oh, yes.' Boysie didn't want to set him off in that direction. It would be embarrassing to explain; now, after all these years.

'You come far?' he asked, for something to say.

'London.'

'London, that's nice.'

'Very nice,' agreed Mostyn, looking damnably supercilious. Boysie waited. Mostyn was drumming his fingers on the desk.

'Well, sir, what was it...'

'You want to know why I'm here.' The smile was the one usually reserved for small children, chronic invalids and advanced cases of senility. 'Of course you do.' Mostyn took a slim passport-like folder from his inside pocket and tossed it to Boysie:

'You'd better have a look at those first. Tell you who I am. Identify me. They say we're all searching for our identity these days, don't they? I carry mine with me. Easier in the long run.'

Boysie opened the folder and looked at the cards, clean behind celluloid.

'That one's my General Security Identification,' continued Mostyn, leaning back and looking pleased. 'The other's a Special Branch Warrant Card on loan from Scotland Yard – just to make it easier for me to find out about you.' He stressed the 'you'.

Boysie looked up: natural alarm in his face.

'Don't worry though, old Boysie,' said Mostyn, 'all your secrets are safe with me – the girl in that rating office: even your boss's wife. Tcht, tcht, tcht!'

'What the hell?'

'Don't worry.' Melodic. Soothing.

'What the hell's all this about?' Boysie dimly remembered the salad days in the Council Office. Mostyn looked at him as though trying to decide the best angle of attack. Two cars passed along the road outside, and somewhere, across the fields, a dog barked four times. Eventually, he opted on the frontal approach:

'I've come to offer you a job, Boysie. Something that we think you will do rather well.'

'A job? Me? What kind of job?' Boysie was smiling – a sort of bewildered, nervous convulsion of the mouth.

'With our Department.'

This must be some kind of joke. It was ridiculous: suddenly to be confronted by a man you haven't seen for twelve years (and then only for a few minutes), who waltzes in, gives you a nasty look, and offers you a job with some secret Government department.

Mostyn continued: 'I'll give it to you straight, old boy. We want you to kill for us.'

Boysie was almost struck dumb. He's off his little curly chump, he thought: 'To ... to WHAT?'

'To kill for us.' Mostyn's tone was casual as a crumpled sweater. 'I thought it might appeal to you.'

'Struth, thought Boysie, I'd better do something about this fellow. Mothers' Union coach parties I can cope with; but a nut case...

'Who ... who do I have to kill?'

'People.'

Boysie took a deep breath: 'Look, Colonel Mostyn. Sir! How about a nice cup o' tea? You've been working hard lately, haven't you?'

Mostyn's face went pink, his mouth set in a hard line. When he spoke the drawl was replaced by a clipped sharpness:

'Oakes, anything I say to you in this room must be regarded as absolutely confidential. Do you understand? I haven't got time to fool around.' There was a terrible authority about the man. Boysie remembered the official documents.

'All right,' he said.

'And you needn't start trying to play funny beggars with me. I'm like the two copulating maggots, Oakes – in Dead Earnest. Dead Earnest!' He sounded it.

It wasn't a game. This grotesque conversation was for real: for keeps:

'You want *me*...' Boysie tapped his chest with the forefinger of his right hand, '...to kill...' finger across the throat, '...for *you?*' finger pointed at Mostyn.

Mostyn nodded:

'That's the general idea. Not for me personally, of course. For the Department – for the Government.'

'Why me?' On the fringes of the absurdity, Boysie was aware of ice-cubes being rubbed hard up the back of his neck.

'You seem to forget, old lad,' the slow affected speech had returned, 'I've seen you in action. I watched you shoot two men: very prettily.'

'That? Yes, but...'

'But me no buts, Boysie. You enjoyed it. Anyone could tell that you enjoyed it. You were ... cold blooded, as they say in the newspapers. That's the kind of chap we want. Someone not inclined towards squeamishness.'

'Look.' He drew the word out, changing the double-O to a long 'U'. 'Look, Colonel Mostyn, I think I'd better tell you about...' Boysie stopped in mid-sentence. This man had convinced himself. He was never going to believe that the whole thing was a horrible mistake. Somehow Mostyn had got it into his strange London head that he, Boysie, had upped and shot the two Germans without a jot of emotion or tittle of feeling. Worse,

Mostyn imagined that Boysie was perfectly prepared to do it again: and, perhaps, again, and again, and again. Fumbling for an escape, he changed his tactics:

'That happened once, sir: wartime. People do funny things in wartime.'

'You don't think we're still at war?'

Boysie was lost: 'Well, I mean, it's peace, isn't it? I mean, well, I know about the communists and that, but...'

'We're still at war, Boysie, only it's gone underground – until some mad bastard presses the button and we all go sailing on the big mushroom. Think of me...' He was leaning forward, confidentially, choosing his words like a parson acting some well-rehearsed ad lib illustration from the pulpit: 'Think of me as a recruiting officer. I'm asking you to take the Queen's shilling. To enlist. You'd be a soldier again: an officer this time. Not in uniform, of course; and, I might add, you would be paid a consider-able amount of money. The country needs you, Boysie.'

He went on, but Boysie stuck on the word 'money'. I wonder, he thought, what they would offer? He couldn't face the idea of killing anyone, but there was money around: and he needed the filthy lucre PDQ. Mostyn was still talking:

'...so you would only be killing as a soldier kills – for Queen and country: under orders.

We'd train you, of course. It's really a challenge.'

Boysie wondered about the best way to lead the conversation back to cash:

'Er ... enemy agents, spies and that? That's who you'd want me to...'

'Liquidate is the word that's evading you. Yes. We'll want you to arrange a few accidents. There will be fatalities ... to people on the other side. Got to keep the coroners busy, old Boysie; got to keep their hands in for the big one.'

'You mentioned money...'

'Ah, now you're talking. You know, I believe it's going to be a pleasure doing business with you Boysie. I think we're going to become quite good chums.'

When the full scale of salary and conditions was laid in front of him, Boysie – staggered at the government's generosity – knew he would be insane not to take the risk. You weren't offered money like this every day of the week. He even became quite confident about coping with the work. At the Espionage School – with its quiet professionalism, stately home atmosphere, hidden firing ranges and lecture rooms which hummed with confidential information – he regained pride in physical fitness, enjoyed perfecting his marksmanship, and marvelled at the general ingenuity of the organisation.

Occasionally, there were twinges of conscience: sudden moments when heart and stomach sank as he remembered the bitter end for which he was being trained. He was still unable to picture himself performing the actual act of execution, but time was on his side, and, he thought, maybe, when the moment came, dealing in death might not be so bad. He tried to cultivate the detachment of a surgeon: thinking of those who were to be his victims, as spreading cancers which had to be removed.

Yet, as the weeks swept by, the anxieties became more pronounced. Instead of the tiny pinpricks of worry, he began to suffer whole days of depression and nights of restless uneasiness. Life in London, under Mostyn's comprehensive instruction, brought about a deceptive change. He could almost see himself becoming an indolent dilettante; a leisurely man-about-town. His personality, his whole outlook, was undergoing a subtle alteration: to the extent that he began to despise his past. Occasionally, he went as far as inventing a fictitious background – complete with country seat – for the benefit of impressionable young women.

Then the time came, towards the end of his training, when he was forced to think hard about the duties which, all-too-soon, would rest on his shoulders and spread their blood-stained tendrils into his mind. Mostyn arranged several exercises – dummy runs, in which Boysie, now commissioned with the code-letter 'L', was briefed on a target and called upon to work out the kill in detail. He didn't mind concentrating on the overall plan; but the mere thought of having to carry it out turned his bowels to jelly.

Boysie finally came to the conclusion that – having reached the point of no return – he was doomed. The simple undeniable fact haunted him: he was emotionally incapable of carrying the operation to its murderous conclusion. But it was too late; he was too involved, and there was no way of escape: either from Mostyn or himself.

The first one came only four days after Mostyn announced that Boysie was now on permanent standby. The telephone rang at about nine in the morning:

'"L"?' said the voice.

'Yes?'

'Number Two. Pressure. This is a live assignment, come round, will you.'

The briefing room was hidden behind an innocuous tobacconists in the Edgware Road. The target was a woman: Frances Ann Chandler: age thirty-seven: working at the War Office. Boysie spent the morning watching motion pictures of her, taken secretly as she arrived and left her work. In the afternoon he studied a twenty-page dossier which plotted her habitual routine –

including the information that she travelled daily from Surbiton to Waterloo on the 8.56 a.m, and from Waterloo to Surbiton on the 6.7p.m. By six o'clock, he knew the girl about as well as if he had been sleeping with her. He was conversant with her mannerisms, favourite kinds of chocolate and cigarettes; could tell you where she bought her clothes and was familiar with her taste in literature. The whole thing was very disturbing: for Boysie found himself liking the portrait of Frances Ann Chandler which the report painted for him.

'A railway tragedy strikes me as being your best bet, old boy,' said Mostyn as he was leaving the room. 'See you when it's all over. No hurry; anytime this week. Best of luck, Boysie.'

The next morning, he was up early, driving to Surbiton to make visual contact with the target. He took the train back to Waterloo, riding in the same compartment as Miss Chandler, and realised that the game was up. For one thing, Frances Chandler was a very attractive woman. She had even given him an undoubtedly sensual smile as he stood aside to let her leave the train at Waterloo. What was worse, she reminded him of one of the girls he had known in the old Bird Sanctuary days. Even if she had been plotting to atomise the whole of the southern counties, he could never bring himself to kill this girl: it was out of the question. People, thought Boysie, didn't just go out and kill other people. He couldn't do it: it wasn't his line.

That night he had three goes at telephoning Mostyn: his nerve failing on each occasion. He wanted to hang on to the flat, the life, the salary and the new darling little regiment of women he had collected. To do this he would have to dispose of Miss Frances Ann Chandler – and that wouldn't be the end; there would be others.

The brainwave came after his sixth large whisky: around three in the morning. Ironically, it was Mostyn himself who had provided the answer. During his London training, Boysie had been taken on regular familiarisation jaunts round the night-clubs – from the plushy playboy joints to the seedy dubious dives of the West End. About a month previously they had gone to *The Strangulated Tortoise:* a club which, as Mostyn had warned him, was openly regarded as one of the favourite underworld clearing houses.

The Strangulated Tortoise was a dark, and not particularly hygienic, cellar off one of the narrow, suspicious alleys which run, like warrens, between Beak and Brewer Streets, in what the tourist guide-books call: 'London's colourful Soho.' A dance floor, the size of a largish dustbin lid, was circled by tables pushed well back out of the light, and after midnight the atmosphere took on the appearance of some smogbound island. Music blared from a hidden juke box, and, twice nightly, four of the girls from a neighbouring strip club, tottered in lethargically divested themselves of what little clothing they were wearing, and teetered out again – much to the delight of the raucous clientele who paid £2 a head cover charge, for the entertainment.

'Shouldn't think she's got much stamina in bed,' said Mostyn, looking disenchantedly at an anaemic blonde who had just removed *le minimum* and now stood naked, but for a pair of leather boots and a riding crop. Mostyn looked round:

'Do you know, old boy, I could get your job done, for a fraction of what it's costing us, just by mentioning it to the headwaiter of this dump? Makes you think, doesn't it?'

'Why don't you then?'

'No go. The Chief has an aversion to using the criminal element. Wants a home-grown professional practised in our ways of procedure. But, honestly, Boysie, you could get your grandmother carved into little pieces for less than a couple of hundred quid. See the chap sitting over there – one with the glasses? Thin type?'

'Yes.'

'Dare say he'd fix us up. Cute bird, only been done for petty larceny. But we know different. Very clever is our Mr Griffin.'

Now, on the brink of his initial mission, Boysie remembered the nondescript, grey, hornrimmed Griffin. Perhaps he was the answer to the macabre problem.

Three days later, Griffin agreed to a meeting – in the Bridge Street Lyons under the shadow of Big Ben.

'Sorry to have kept you waiting, guv'nor, but I has to be a bit careful – bloke in my trade.' He had cracked and broken fingernails, Boysie noted, and a handpainted tie which simply screeched at his shirt: a man of fifty-odd, who might have been a private, lurking, detective, or a sly summons server.

'That's all right, Mr Griffin,' said Boysie, looking over his shoulder – a habit which took some time to conquer.

'Well, you seem to be "clean" – I had a couple of the boys check you out. I'm always a bit chary of the police, and those bloody newspaper men.'

'Of course.' Boysie sipped his tea.

'Now, guv'nor, what can I do for you?' Griffin's voice had a rough throatiness: as though it had been hoarsened crying wares in a street market.

'I believe you … er … dispose of people.' Boysie consciously put on Mostyn's drawl.

'Yes, we can arrange that.' He paused, aware of Boysie's uneasiness: I've been in the business a long time, Mr Oakes, so you needn't be embarrassed with me. I've ceased to wonder at the foolishness of my fellow men.'

'Oh!' The homespun philosophy took him by surprise.

'Started as an undertaker,' continued Griffin. 'So got used to the inevitability of it all quite early on. Who d'you want done? Mother-in-law?'

'Well, there'll probably be more than one...'

'Don't you fret about that, guv'nor – I never ask any questions so long as the lolly's right: and I can promise you, sir, that everything'll be in the best of taste. I mean, undertaking taught me that. A bit religious, I am, guv'nor, on the quiet like.'

Frances Ann Chandler departed from this vale of tears, suddenly at Surbiton Station, the following evening. In fact, there wasn't very much left of Miss Chandler by the time the live rail and the mincemeat wheels of the train had done for her. Griffin's elbow, unexpected and hard in her ribs, had toppled her from the platform before she even had time to cry out or realise what was happening to her.

Mostyn parodied:

'Frances Ann has gone to rest
Safe at last on Abraham's breast,
Which may be rough on Frances Ann,
But it's certainly sexy for Abraham.'

It was so easy. He even became quite friendly with Griffin, and together they worked out a regular format. After a briefing, there would be a telephone call; then a meeting in Lyons. Boysie would travel to wherever the kill was to be made, Griffin never far behind; and once Boysie had put the finger on the target, Griffin would take over – with excellent, though fatal, results. It was even relatively simple for Boysie to blot the more revolting consequences from his mind. This was a game (with his monthly cheque as the stake), in which moral responsibility had to be thrown to the wind.

Early light was beginning to filter into the room. Boysie, still awake, sat in the chair looking, unseeing, at the window. Remembering those first days had helped to lift the depression. For nearly seven years he had successfully foxed the Department. Officially, he was responsible for the liquidation of twenty-five people – all enemies of Britain. Unofficially, and only because of his one weakness – the inability to promiscuously dispense death – he had sub-contracted, at £300 a corpse, plus expenses: a sum which balanced easily against the regular body-bonuses. Damn it, why was he worrying? It was a trick played, commercially, on the government every single day. Sometime, he knew, it would have to end. There was always a certain amount of strain: and of late there had been the neuroses concerning his own mortality. Perhaps this 'Coronet' thing was going to bring on the showdown. Griffin, as always, was his only hope.

Iris stirred, her hand searching for him on the pillow:

'Boysie?'

'All right, sweetie, I'm here.'

'Whatyoudoing?'

'Having a cigarette.'

'Come back to bed, Boysie.' Then softly, 'I want you.'

Boysie had got his second wind, and – in spite of the sleepless night – performed with an expertise and polish, the like of which Iris had never experienced. At last, he relaxed, and, within five minutes, was knocking out a long stream of Zs which, for some time, kept Iris from returning to her satisfied dreams.

In London the milk bottles were rattling and the road-cleaners were out; dawn was shaking the city by the shoulder and Wordsworth was again being proved accurate about Westminster Bridge. An irritated Mostyn, unshaven and barely awake, stumped into the Operations' Room.

'Sorry to get you out so early, Number Two,' said the bland Operations' Officer.

'But you did ask for immediate notification on "L".'

'What's happened to the moron?'

'We've just decoded a message from Blueboy...'

'You fellows and the bloody codebook. I never can remember these people – Blueboy?'

'Our man on the Côte D'Azur.'

'Of course, the pensioned RAF chaplain, yes, I know. What's he say?'

'Apparently "L" had a brush with the opposition last night. He thinks Sheriek was mixed up in it...'

'That stupid fool. I thought they'd got rid of him years ago – the man's like something out of the Comic Cuts.'

'"L" was missing from about 4.45 until 10.30. Came back looking as though he'd escaped from the jaws of death. Blueboy also says there seems to be an opposition flap on. Lots of activity.'

'Does he now? OK, put an extra watch on "L" and we'll see what materialises. Thank you for letting me know – nothing concrete, but ... well, I've got a feeling about this one.'

They were interrupted by a cipher clerk:

'Think you ought to look at this, sir.' He spoke to the Operations' Officer. Out of interest, Mostyn followed them to the map.

'Redland Airforce, Super Security Order,'

said the clerk, putting his finger on the Perspex cover. 'They're prohibiting all of their military flights along this corridor – passing from the coast through Archangel – as from 0900 our time Tuesday. They've also alerted their Number Six Fighter Group – the Arctic Coast boys: on special standby as from Monday night.'

'That's interesting,' said Mostyn. 'Keep me informed, will you.' Something was up, he could smell it. Things would break soon – unpleasant things, and very soon.

7 – *CÔTE D'AZUR*

Sunday June 9th 1963

QUADRANT

The mistral – that dry northerly wind which whips down the Rhone valley to collide with the hot Mediterranean air in the Gulf of Lyons – can be one of life's hardships on the Côte D'Azur. It blows for days on end; flaying the nerves, shifting bathers from the beaches, overturning tables, ruining soigné hairstyles, sprinkling sand and dust into the eyes, bowling hats along the broad streets and rippling the bright awnings outside the promenade bars. With it comes a testy, razor-blade edginess which makes even a patient man snap and scratch at his most intimate friends.

The mistral began to blow along the coast just after dawn. Its current shook the palms and lifted the girls' skirts as they hurried to early Mass at the church of St Michel. The café owners looked out, shrugged their shoulders, and turned down the corners of their mouths. The sea started to churn, sending great breakers clawing, with a sputter of

173

soapsud foam, against the rocks – splattering the promenade, drowning the Sunday churchbells. Tourists emerged resigning themselves to a day off the beaches. The sun was hot and rising, the wind unpleasant. Boysie Oakes dreamed of faded blondes lashing at a pile of old rags with riding crops, while Mostyn, clad only in a green jock-strap, puffed at a black cheroot and watched from a blue deck-chair. Boysie always dreamed in technicolour.

'Wake up, lazy!' said Mostyn. 'Wake up!' Only it wasn't Mostyn.

'Boysie! Wake up!' said Iris.

He stretched and opened one eye. She was standing at the foot of the bed, dizzying in petal-white brassiere and panties which frilled out in a ruffle of nylon. Iris was about to dip her head into a bright, patterned shirt-dress.

'Don't put it on, sweetie, you'll spoil the picture,' said Boysie, comfortable and indolent. 'Come over here.'

'You're a lazy bastard. Anyway, we haven't time, darling: it's gone ten-thirty already. Damn, now see what you've made me do. Trying to wake you up, I haven't put my slip on.'

She dropped the dress on to the bed and slithered into the tailored slip, zipping it up the side in a way which made Boysie squirm with pleasure:

'You'd be a wow in a strip show.'

'Mm!' Iris pouted a cat-licking-the-cream look: 'Tell you something, love: I think I'm a bit kinky that way. I'm always getting urges to take off my clothes in public. I've been standing here stark naked for ten minutes trying to wake you.'

'Good for you. It's the full narcissus thing, you know. Hasn't got anything to do with the other. Once talked to a stripper – she was nineteen, came from Bootle and thought she had the most beautiful body since Venus. Wasn't interested in sex. Just wanted to display herself. Even offered to pose next to some statues in the British Museum: but they turned her down. Pity really; she'd have filled the place. Ouoogrrough!' He yawned. 'Did you say something about breakfast?'

Iris was pouring the coffee:

'You have a bad night, love?'

'Honey, I had a fabulous night. Only I didn't sleep too well.'

'Coffee?'

He nodded. Iris brought the cup, put it on the bedside table and perched herself on the edge of the bed, crossing her legs, displaying a pair of eminently strokable knees. She put a hand on Boysie's forehead and rumpled his hair:

'Why the insomnia? Worried? About the operation?'

'I suppose so. We're not all great big

hulking machines, you know.'

'Sure. I know. But you've done lots before. Or is it always like this?'

'In our trade, sweetie, you never get used to it.' He put his hand lightly on her leg, above the knee, underneath her dress:

'Do you know what I specialise in, Iris? Do you know what I do for the Department?'

'You're a courier, aren't you? A Grade One Courier?'

Boysie thought how desirable she looked when she frowned. She was showing concern for him. Perhaps that's what he needed: someone to be concerned about him: not just a bird to get into bed with; on whom to test his agility and capacity; to provide him with kicks: but a girl who would worry about him.

'Yes, I'm a kind of courier,' he said.

'It's a rather special kind, though: isn't it?'

'Ah!' Yes, he thought, it's rather special: so bloody special that I can't even do it. It's got special sets of psychiatric disorders, all built-in and ticking like mad. He sat up, kissed her on the nose, and rapidly turned his attention to the coffee.

Boysie was still lying back in bed when Iris left for Nice by taxi at eleven-fifteen. He rang down to the restaurant and ordered lunch for three, to be sent up at one o'clock. Then he prepared to pass the time by steeping himself in a warm bath. As he got out of bed, his foot caught in Iris's lime nightdress – dropped to the floor during the straining perspiration of the early hours. Boysie wondered if there would ever be another chance. The niggling neuroses again began to teem inside him. As he turned on the bath taps, he noticed that his hands were shaking.

The hands of the electric clock in the airport lounge stood steady at noon. Iris, waiting with a long, iced Pernod, dropped the copy of *Vogue* into her lap, unhitched the dark-framed glasses from her ears and looked towards the entrance.

The man stood there for a moment, his eyes following a precise pattern as he scanned the whole lounge, examining every face. He saw her and came quickly across, weaving through the waiting passengers. Iris tilted her chin, looking up with an expression of restrained amusement, her eyebrows arched questioningly. He leaned towards her:

'Coronet,' said the man.

'And ermine to you.' Iris smiled. 'Nice to see you again. Come on ... Quadrant.' They both laughed, as though embroiled in some childish plot.

'I've hired a car. Thought it would make things easier,' said Quadrant.

'Clever you.' Iris took his arm, and, like

two old friends, they walked, in step, chatting from the lounge.

Sheriek was bored: lonely in the villa now the others had gone. After they had cleared up the mess on the previous evening, he had sent Yacob and Gregory off to Sospel. It was better than keeping them cooped up in the villa. They were out of the way up there: high in the mountains, in the ancient little town perched like a nest among the rocks. They had friends in Sospel: they would be able to drink; perhaps there would be women. They would be safe until he needed them again. Sheriek wished he had a woman in the villa now. He had nearly rung Cannes that morning but decided against it in case the Co-ordinator arrived.

He didn't hear the car. The first he knew of the visitors was the sudden tin-tinkle of the old bell echoing through the silent house. They were standing in the porch when he came through to the hall, mopping his brow with a spotless handkerchief:

'Yes? Can I help you?'

'Baudelaire?'

'Oh... Yes... Yes!' Sheriek was surprised. He stood looking at the pair, impassive, framed in the doorway.

'You are Chekhov?'

'I am Chekhov,' said the Co-ordinator.

'We'd like to talk to you,' said the other.

'Of course. Come in. Come in. I've been expecting you.' He ushered them into the hall: rather like a madame in a brothel, thought the Co-ordinator.

'We have much to discuss. You have not done well, Baudelaire. You have been a great disappointment to us...' Acid in the Co-ordinator's voice.

'I can explain all that. It's really the idiots who were working for me...'

'We'll hear about it in a moment,' the Co-ordinator cut in.

As they passed into the florid dining-room, the Co-ordinator's companion casually slid his right hand into his jacket pocket. The fingers closed round a small automatic pistol.

'You'd like a drink, I'm sure,' oiled Sheriek.

'We would love a drink,' smiled the Co-ordinator.

'First, we would love a drink,' said the other one.

Quadrant had big ears. They stood out like little plastic scoops stuck to the sides of his head. The ears fascinated Boysie; they gave the man an unearthly look; a Martian look: if you pushed them forward, and stuck them down, they would act as blinkers, he thought.

Boysie had not really taken to Quadrant.

The courier had that superior attitude which Boysie often detected in the breed. The manner was a bit 'young Guards'; plum-purée voices; high-powered cars; daring pints supped dangerously after hours – no end of a lark, what? – and pink, 'daddy-says', debs, who would probably surprise you by passing on a virulent dose of the clap. The roots of this last thought came from a recent conversation with a doctor, who had told Boysie that venereal disease was more prevalent in Chelsea than anywhere else in London.

Quadrant, Boysie decided, was a chinless wonder of the first water. Moreover, he had been sloppy with his food; slobbered over the chicken and tomato consommé; picked disgustingly at the filet de boeuf a l'amiral; turned his nose up at the crème a l'orange, and was now cutting great hunks off the roquefort, stuffing them into his mouth like a guzzling child with a bag of jelly-babies. A right schmuck, thought Boysie. I wonder what stone Mostyn found this one under?

'Prefer a simple meal at lunchtime meself,' said Quadrant through a cheese-speckled spray.

Boysie thought it was time to deal with this burke. Pushing back his chair, he selected a panatella without offering them to Quadrant – lit it, and blew a thin column of smoke across the table into the courier's face:

'You've got some stuff for me, I believe?' said Boysie. Quadrant's behaviour had temporarily exorcised all fear. 'I'd like to get down to work if you don't mind. Anyway, you'll have to be getting back soon, won't you?'

'No hurry, chum. Not at the moment, anyway.' Quadrant seemed to be constructed of alligator skin. 'All in good time. It's going to take us the best part of the afternoon, anyway.' He smiled, almost benignly: first at Iris, who had been silent since the consommé; then at Boysie:

'If I were you, "L" – isn't it silly not being able to use our proper names? If I were you, I'd get this table cleared. I've got lots of pretty maps and photos for you to look at.'

Damn the man, thought Boysie. He got up and went over to the service bell. Before he could press it, Quadrant was off again:

'Wait a minute, though. We've got a job for the little lady first.' He turned his beam on to Iris again, ears flapping out charm signals:

'We can call you by your name, can't we, Iris, old thing? Well you aren't allowed to stay in here while I'm briefing the boy friend – he'll put you in the picture later on. You mustn't be told *all*, you know. In the meantime...' He practically sang the last three words, pausing, as if about to make a statement of great importance. 'In the meantime

181

'... you can be of enormous help.'

'Just say the word.' Iris was at about the same position on her tether as Boysie.

'Your return flight is booked for Tuesday, isn't it?'

They agreed.

'Surprise. You're going back tomorrow. On the afternoon flight: BE.105: half-past three. So, if Iris trips along to Cooks – straight up the road here, to the right; then turn left, it's on the right-hand side, you can't miss it – they will make the necessary alterations. It's all laid on, just tell them what you want. Will you do that for me? Good girl.'

Boysie and Iris looked at each other – Boysie hoping that they were having identical thoughts: that at least they had tonight together.

When Iris – clutching the passports and tickets – had left for Cooks, Boysie rang for room service, sat down with his back to Quadrant and waited in irritated silence. Quadrant, unperturbed by the obvious snub, sauntered on to the balcony, planted his buttocks on the guard-rail, and looked up at the mountains, now wreathed in grey cloud-caps. The wind, coming in from the shore, agitated his thin sandy hair, which he kept smoothing back with a fin-like hand.

When the waiters had cleared the luncheon debris, Quadrant returned to the room, picked up his briefcase, which had been lying on the bed throughout the meal, and pulled a chair up to the table. Boysie followed suit. The two men faced each other as though the chips were down and this was the start of a cut-throat game. Quadrant unlocked the case, took out a thin, cream envelope and tossed it to Boysie. Boysie picked it up as though it was impregnated with some rare deadly virus. Type-written across the front in red, were the words: 'Target L26. Top Secret. Destroy.' He glanced up: Quadrant was watching him like a psychiatrist evaluating a patient's reaction to some trick test. Boysie slit open the envelope, withdrew the photograph and looked at it. A few hundred volts seemed to shoot through him. Boysie visibly recoiled:

'Christ... But it's...'

The photograph stared back at him unblinking, good-natured: the internationally famous face: lean, sharp, and very, very important.

'That's it, "L". That's your boy.'

'But it's the Duke of...'

'Quite.'

'Prin...'

'Precisely.'

Boysie stood up:

'What's the game, Quadrant? Who's trying to be funny?'

Quadrant interlaced his fingers, pushed back with his heels, and rocked the chair on to its rear legs. For about five seconds, he looked gravely at Boysie's perplexed face. Then, he threw back his head and exploded in a rumble of turbulent laughter:

'Oh dear … your face… Number Two said to watch your face…'

'Look, mate!' Boysie's temper was on the verge of collapse. 'If you don't shut up and give me the lowdown, you're going to get a swift punch up the Bradshaw!'

'Calm down, "L"… Oh dear… It's only that Number Two said he'd give a month's pay to see your face when I showed you the target… Oh, dearie me, sport…'

Boysie was still not amused:

'I am not going to bump any royalty,' he said in a tone of an offended dowager.

'Nor are you, sport. It's all right: I'll explain.' Quadrant's mirth was abating.

'I should bloody-well think so. The Duke! Come on, let's have the real one.'

Quadrant began to splutter again:

'But you've got him, sport. He is your target– No! Wait a minute. Sit down.' Boysie had moved menacingly towards him. Quadrant spoke rapidly:

'He's in on this. The Duke's in on it. It's not a pukka operation: it's a security exercise.'

'Oh Gawd, not one of those,' moaned Boysie, thinking of the wasted time and effort.

'We're all going to have a game of spies and assassins. It'll be great fun really.'

'I'm glad you think so.' The whole of his short connubial weekend well nigh ruined for the sake of a perishing security exercise. Then the brighter side of the picture appeared, floodlit, coloured and accompanied by a fanfare from the Royal College of Music. No kill. He was safe. Griffin wouldn't be needed. Reprieve.

'Sit down,' said Quadrant, 'and I'll put you in the picture.' Boysie lit another panatella and sat.

'For some time,' began Quadrant, 'RAF Security have been on to us to run a check on their boys at Gayborough. Know it?'

'Warwickshire, isn't it? Somewhere in the Midlands.'

'That's it. V-bombers and a bit of secret stuff. Not much, but enough to warrant maximum security effort.' He wrinkled his nose. 'Do you have to smoke those foul things? Don't know how the girlie stands 'em.'

'You leave the girlie to me.'

'OK, sport. Just trying to be helpful. You know – even his best friend wouldn't, and all that rot.'

'Get on with it.'

Quadrant shrugged. 'All right. To be brief; the Duke is paying a call there on Tuesday – incidentally, that's TS as well: no press, no

185

release, no information, silent as a tomb. Number Two thinks it'd be an ideal time to test their reactions and have fun at the RAF's expense. He's arranged for a red warning to be put out on the visit. So they'll know something's up.' He smiled blandly. 'But they won't know that the Duke is going to be assassinated right on their own front door. Think of it, sport. Isn't it a wheeze? Typical of Number Two – give 'em a real touch of the screaming diarrhoea.'

'Bloody strip cartoon. Very droll,' said Boysie, still rankled at the thought of being put in jeopardy because Mostyn wanted to play cops and robbers with the RAF.

'Don't be such a square. We're going to bring a ray of sunshine into a lot of dull little service lives. The Duke's mad about the idea. Thinks it's no end of a lark – Outward Bound and all that.'

'Save us,' said Boysie, lifting his eyes to heaven.

Quadrant took a neat pile of papers from the case and leaned, confidentially, across the table:

'Now here's the dope.' The atmosphere became less tense. 'You fly back with the girl-friend tomorrow afternoon. You get to London Central at 18.20. Number Two says that, in view of the fact that you are out of the country, he might possibly enlarge the exercise. Keep the airport ladies on their toes. He was just the weeniest bit acid about you and the girlie, by the way…'

'Do you mind?'

'All right. Just a friendly warning. But the airport boys might be on the look out. So we'll have to move a bit sharpish – through customs like a dose of senna. I'll meet you outside – passenger exit – into the car and away.'

He spread out a section of map. A route was marked, in red, from London airport to the dot that was Gayborough. Quadrant ran his finger along the bright line:

'You can see we're going to take the long way round.'

Boysie nodded: 'Bloody London to Manchester by the Isle of Wight.'

'We'll stop for dinner in Oxford. Linger there a while and then proceed, very slowly, up here to Gayborough.'

'How many're in this?'

'Only you, the driver, me and the girl. She's a bit of a dead weight now, but we'll have to take her along for the ride. She can look after your case, take it back to town – put it in your flat or something. OK?'

'OK.'

'On the last lap,' he was still tracing the route on the map. 'We dress you up – in the back of the car: fit you out with a sniper's smock, black-face make-up, all that jazz; compass, and the rifle…'

'What am I using?' Boysie had long schooled himself to ask pertinent questions during a briefing.

'An old Lee Enfield Mark III – modified, of course … 303 with a Tasco variable power scope and camera attachment. That's very important. Number Two wants your shots recorded for the RAF people's debriefing. You'll have one magazine with the rifle – five rounds – and two spare clips. Blank ammunition, of course, but it's *got* to be heard – the Duke's got to hear it.'

'OK.' You had to take your hat off to Mostyn. When he made up his mind to rip something apart he did it with relish, and thought of everything.

Quadrant opened another map. This time a large plan of RAF Gayborough and the surrounding area. Clipped to the top corner were a set of air-to-ground and ground-to-ground photographs.

'At about 03.00 on Tuesday morning we drop you … here.' He indicated a point on what appeared to be a secondary road running parallel to, and about two miles from the main road which passed along the airfield's western boundary.

'You can see from the photographs that you're going to be in dead ground. There's a slight rise, from the main Gayborough road, which drops down to this one. We'll give you a compass bearing when you leave the car:

follow that, and it should bring you up the rise to these trees, here.'

Boysie scrutinised the map and pictures. The photographs showed that the knot of about four trees lay uphill, in a direct line with the main gate – about half-a-mile of open ground between trees and gate.

'Plenty of cover there. Nobody's going to spot you. You'll be snug as a corpse in a coffin. View's good too: see everything: great big aeroplanes taking off and landing; airmen marching – real show of strength.'

'I can't wait.'

'Tell you what. You can have some great games with the telescopic sight. I had binoculars when I was up there casing the job; the married quarters – over to the right there – provide some very high-class entertainment first thing in the morning: bedroom windows. Do you know, the Groupie's wife wears baby doll pyjamas?'

'Disgusting.'

'True.'

'Look, let's get on, huh? Let's hear the whole of it.'

'About the Groupie's wife?'

'About the exercise. About Coronet. I don't want to be at it all day.'

'If you say so, sport.'

Boysie couldn't remember when one man had irritated him so much. He made a mental note to speak to Mostyn about it;

then remembered, with a kick of conscience, that Mostyn probably wanted a few sharp words with him – about Iris.

Quadrant continued: 'You should be in position by 04.00; and there you stay until 11.00. We'll give you some coffee and sandwiches; there's a nice bank you can snuggle behind. But don't go to sleep.'

'I'm not likely to. I am experienced, you know.' Boysie was putting on a fairish show of efficiency.

'At 11.00 the Duke's car will arrive. It'll pull up here.' He stabbed at the main gate. 'He will get out to inspect the guard. As he walks from the car, you put two bullets into him – metaphorically speaking, of course. But, for heaven's sake, don't forget that you have a camera in the sight. Number Two is most anxious that the film should show an accurate aim on the Duke. So play it like for real, sport.'

Boysie grunted.

'The Duke's been completely briefed, and he'll be listening for the shots. He's going to stagger and fall as soon as he hears them – giving it the full business. Number Two says he made quite a crack about getting Larry Olivier or Peter Hall down to direct him.'

'I should have thought Cheyenne was his man for this one,' said Boysie dryly. 'What happens next?'

'You play it by ear. The object of the

exercise is to test their security reaction to a ginormous emergency; but you've got nothing to worry about. Number Two'll be there to make sure they don't lose their heads. He'll stop 'em loosing off live ammunition or anything.'

'I should hope so. Where will you be?'

'At 11.00 on Tuesday?'

'Uh-huh.'

'Just going into Hatchetts for my morning livener, I should think. We skiddaddle back to town once we've dropped you. You clear on everything?'

'Think so.'

'Right – let's go over it once more for luck.'

Step by step they retraced the exercise. Then, following the routine procedure, Boysie answered a series of random questions flung at him, with infuriating trickiness, by Quadrant. At last the courier was satisfied:

'I think we've got this one in the bag, sport.'

'You'll be wanting to get along now,' Boysie said happily. Iris was taking her time, and he didn't want Quadrant around when she returned.

'As it happens, I do. But it's not quite as easy as that.'

Quadrant had been wandering round the room in search of a receptacle in which they could burn the papers marked with the red

'Destroy' notation. Finally, he picked on a small metal waste-bin. He put the bin on the table and Boysie joined him to help in the destruction of the photographs and maps.

'Better sign the old blood chitty first,' said Quadrant, taking out the familiar pink form which, cleanly and painlessly, passed the responsibility from one agent to the next whenever an operation was planned orally. At the top, Mostyn had written his precise signature, showing he was satisfied that Quadrant fully understood the instructions. Quadrant had signed – a squirl of initials. Now, he again made his mark and handed the paper and pen to Boysie.

'Let's finish it then,' said Boysie, executing a flourish with the pen, returning the form, and taking up one of the maps. They began to tear the documents, dropping the little paper snowstorm into the container.

'Now, what about last night's fracas?' The question was framed casually.

A set of small, rather sharp, claws sank into Boysie's guts. Blast Iris, he thought. She had no right to mention anything to this ginger-haired wet.

'How did you hear about that?'

Quadrant was in the act of setting light to the miniature bonfire. 'Message from London – before I made contact this morning. Unfortunately, they say I've got to check the damn thing out.' The flame flared violently from the waste-bin. 'And I simply must get back to London tonight. Most inconsiderate of you, getting involved like this.'

Boysie wound up his last ounce of self-control:

'Look, cocker,' he said, using his 'intimidating' voice: 'I didn't ask to get coshed, doped and shot at. It just bloody happened.'

'Bounced you on the old bean, did they?' Quadrant wiped his eyes: 'I say, that jolly thing's smoking a bit, isn't it?'

A thick cloud of particularly acrid smoke was beginning to belch from the waste-bin. It rose to the ceiling, spread out, and then – drawn by the warm air – began to stream through the balcony window.

'It's those damn maps – the paper they use,' said Quadrant, vainly trying to disperse the growing black cumulus by fanning it with his limp hand. The room was overhung with a film of grimy mist:

'We're going to ruin this table.' Boysie attempted to pick up the bin, burning his fingers: jumping back and putting his hand to his mouth with an 'Ouch!' of pain.

They were suddenly aware of shouts from the street below, followed by voices in the passage. The door burst open (Quadrant's hand dipping for his hip pocket). In cannoned a tubby under-manager, clutching a large, crimson fire extinguisher. Through the haze, Boysie could make out the faces of several guests gathered round the door. Cries of *'Pompier'* were coming from down the hall.

'Attention, Messieurs...' puffed the rotund official, elbowing Boysie and Quadrant out of the way and aiming the extinguisher like a bazooka. Before they could stop him, the fearless amateur fireman had let fly with the deflamer. A thin, powerful stream of soapy foam gushed from the appliance at the speed of a rocket exhaust. The bin was lifted straight off the table and out on to the balcony, clattering against the guard-rail and distributing a swarm of charred, sodden piece of paper as it went.

By this time, the Frenchman had lost all control of the extinguisher, which jerked about in his hands like a live, filthy-tempered anaconda. The white jet was playing dangerously over the drenched ninon curtains: any minute it would start whipping round the walls. Its operator fought desperately to bring it to heel – leaning back to absorb the hefty recoil. Boysie made a grab at the under-manager in a frantic effort to redirect the fountain straight out of the balcony window. He slipped, grabbed again, fell headlong and brought both of them crashing to the floor, the extinguisher sandwiched between them. They rolled over, coming to rest against the foot of the bed. An expression of amazed incredulity crossed Boysie's face. He was experiencing a sensation which he had not felt since one humiliating morning when he had disgraced himself at the village school.

It came as something of a relief when he looked down to find that the nozzle of the infernal dousing machine had become lodged in the waistband of his slacks – still spurting the last remnants of its vile, clinging spray. Boysie was up, tentatively shaking his legs. Standing in the now crowded doorway, looking down at him with an expression of long-suffering amusement, was Iris.

'Having fun?' she said.

Mutual explanations and apologies were given and received; tempers were calmed. At last, Iris took charge of a small army of chambermaids bent on erasing all trace of the damage caused by the under-manager's excessive zeal, while Boysie retired to the bathroom to dry off and change. Uninvited, and with his accustomed coolness, Quadrant followed, closing the door behind him. Boysie was engrossed in a long, and venomous spiel against authority:

'Why does it always happen to me? Bleeding people in London: never think of things like this. Stamp "Destroy" over every damn thing regardless of the consequences. Having to burn the stuff in a hotel bedroom!

I ask you? They might have known.' He fumed on: 'Do you know, I nearly choked to death once, trying to consume a photograph marked "Destroy". In Grantham. Temperance Hotel. No matches so had to eat it. Great fat blousy tart she was ... very nearly choked to death.'

He had stripped from the saturated clothes and was rubbing himself violently with a large green bath towel.

'I think it would be more to the point if you told me about last night,' said Quadrant.

'Oh, you still on that blooming business? OK, what do you want to know?'

'Everything. The lot. Tell me the whole sordid tale – words of one syllable if you don't mind.'

Boysie went on towelling. Quadrant moved over to the lavatory pedestal, sat himself on the covered seat and slowly crossed his legs:

'I'm sitting comfortably. You can begin.'

As he finished drying himself, Boysie recapitulated the events of the previous evening – omitting nothing but his intimacy with Coral.

'Charming,' said Quadrant, when the story was done. 'I think we probably know the gent who nabbed you. Between you, me and the wash basin, he's a bit of a twit.'

'I didn't take to him awfully,' said Boysie in a reasonable imitation of Quadrant's plummy voice.

'No? Well, I suppose we'd better go have a look see.'

'What do you mean: "We"?'

'I'm not a clairvoyant, sport. I can't find the place by myself. You'll have to come along and point out the castle where you were thrown into durance vile.'

'I had to fight my way out of that flipping house.' Boysie was becoming nervous again. 'I'm certainly not going to march up there and stick my head right into the flaming lion's mouth again...'

'No one's asking you to stick anything anywhere ... not to my knowledge, anyway,' added Quadrant with a leer. 'You can show me where it is, and I will walk up to the door, ring the bell and say: "I'm the man from the Prudential", or whatever they call it round here. I only want a quick gander so that I can put in a report. You can sit in the car and play patience if you like. You needn't go anywhere near the nasty bad men.'

'My orders are to stay in the hotel.'

'Oh, I forgot,' said Quadrant, with un-ruffled self-satisfaction. 'Number Two says you can finish your little weekend normally – or abnormally if you're so inclined. He's lifted the house-arrest bit. Come along, sport, I've got to catch a jolly old airybuzzer later on.' He looked hard at Boysie who was still only half dressed:

'I say, I rather go for your underwear:

sportin' equipment all over your drawers. Bet that gets the girls, 'specially the archery target...'

'If you're really interested, I've got another pair covered with ants dressed as soldiers,' said Boysie tersely.

'Mm!' said Quadrant. 'Dead contemporary, I bet: red officers with black privates and all that sort of rot. Do hurry, I've got a very heavy date tonight.'

'So have I,' said Boysie from between clenched teeth.

Boysie had not finished his first cigarette when Quadrant returned from the villa. They had driven out along the coast road – squinting enviously, through the afternoon's last slant of sun, at the bathers and bikinied mermaids. These people – and those who inhabited the trim, tidy yachts snug in Monaco harbour – seemed to belong to a different world: a place of laughing normality, unconcerned with the balance of power or the secret war of peace.

He had recognised the iron gates – still open – as soon as he saw them: set back from a bend in the road half-a-mile on the other side of Beaulieu. Quadrant backed the Dauphin into a narrow, walled lane a hundred yards farther up the road, got out and set off with a springy walk for the villa, leaving Boysie cursing to himself and contemplating the unprepossessing view. Quadrant returned:

'You won't mind me asking,' he said, 'but have you been up to your old tricks?'

'Waddyou mean, my old tricks?'

'No.' Quadrant bit his lip. 'You haven't had the opportunity. I think you'd better take a walk up to the Villa Romana with me – that's what it's called: damn great letters over the door: about as tasteless as Chez Nous or Ethelstan.'

'Must I?'

'No need to be scared…'

'You're joking, of course?'

'There's nobody there: oiseaux have flown. But there is something you should see.'

Boysie had slipped the automatic into his trousers pocket before leaving the hotel. Now, it was comforting to hold the cool butt, close to his thigh, as they walked slowly up the sloping drive. The villa was a small, rococo affair washed in pale, uneven pink: two storeys with a wide balcony curving round the south side. The fading cream sun-blinds were down, and, though the door stood open, the place had an uninhabited air – as though the occupants had left suddenly, or been snatched away by some midnight catastrophe. The brass cat still held the door ajar. Boysie began to feel a slight nausea as last night's memories riffled through his mind.

'It's down here,' said Quadrant, leading him to the curtained archway. They descended the stairs.

'I think this is the chap responsible for your little adventure.' Quadrant pushed against the steel door, and Boysie saw the man whom he had glimpsed, standing in the porch next to Gregory, when Coral had died over the bonnet of the Continental.

Sheriek was naked, hanging by his wrists from the *strappado* – arms wrenched from their sockets, broken and twisted like an ill-treated plastic doll: the palms and inside of the elbows turned outwards. In life he had been fat and sleek; now, debased by death, he seemed to have been deflated – the bladder of his stomach punctured by three ragged bullet-holes from which dried blood traced sinewy patterns down the hairy legs.

'Someone didn't like him, did they?' mused Quadrant.

Boysie retched soundlessly, then turned and walked unsteadily up the steps. An eye for an eye, he thought. It was all very well, but his crafty weekend with Iris seemed to have cost two lives already.

Out on the road again, Quadrant looked at his watch:

'I should imagine that the Fat One got his because he let you escape: so you will be careful, won't you? Number Two's very keen that nothing should go wrong on Tuesday –

even though it's only an exercise.'

'Go to hell,' said Boysie with some feeling.

'I'm afraid I've got to go to Nice,' smiled Quadrant, again peeping at his watch. 'Post haste too, old sport. Got to return this bus for one thing. 'Fraid I won't be able to take you all the way back to Menton...'

'I bet you and Mostyn get on like a flaming house...'

'Yes. Tell you what. I'll run you up to Beaulieu station. Plenty of trains from there. Be back in no time.'

Boysie waited for nearly an hour and a half at the tiny, sun-baked station before he was able to board a train for Menton.

The Co-ordinator had been waiting for the telephone to ring:

'Yes?' said the Co-ordinator.

'Just wanted to let you know that he fell for the whole thing.'

'Good. I didn't anticipate any trouble.'

'He imagines it's all been planned by his own people. Just as we said.'

'He'll be sorry.'

'Surprise for the Duke too.' There was a pause.

'He has also been shown the remains of our other friend.'

'That should give him something to think about.'

'A salutary lesson.'

'I shall see you tomorrow then, as arranged.'

'Very good. As arranged.' The Co-ordinator replaced the receiver and smiled. The operation, planned so carefully over the past twelve months, was coming to its climax.

That night, in the bridal suite of the Hotel Miramont, Boysie and Iris made love four times – a satisfactory conclusion to their obstacle-strewn weekend. On Monday morning they swam, from the small spit of sand which borders Garavan harbour in Menton's old quarter. They lunched, quietly, at the hotel, packed and prepared to take Flight BE.105 from Nice to London.

8 – *ENGLAND*

Monday June 10th 1963

CORONET

The old throbbing fears about flying returned while Boysie and Iris were having their morning swim. Dread loomed even larger over lunch, and by the time Boysie was ready to leave for the airport, he had reached his usual state of pure chicken-hearted funk. Now it was even worse for he had no excuse to travel separately from Iris. So Boysie resorted to the oldest courage-booster known to man: eau de vie – neat brandy taken in exorbitant quantities.

After lunch he drank seven in a row, and purchased a half-bottle which appeared from his hip pocket as soon as they were settled in the taxi.

'You're knocking it back a bit, aren't you?' said Iris.

'Just a little drinkie, sweetie. Keep the spirits up. Drown the sorrows – leavin' this Gallic paradise. Have one.'

'No thank you. Go easy, though, Boysie, don't get sloshed.' She looked at him, realising that the warning was already too late. The half-bottle had diminished to a quarter.

'You know they can refuse to let you get on to an aeroplane if you're sloshed...'

'Whiz Oh!'

'...Happened to a cousin of mine in Madrid.'

'Ole!'

'And don't forget you've got a job of work to do. We're in enough trouble already. Mostyn'll be furious if you're tight when we get to London.'

'Bugger Mostyn.'

'Oh, Boysie, you're hopeless!'

Boysie began to chuckle to himself. The chuckle turned into a full-bellied laugh.

'All right then, what is it? You're obviously dying to tell me.'

'Jusht thought of somethin' very funny 'bout Moshtyn...'

'Well?'

'Moshtyn'sh...' Another breaker of breathless chuckling. '...Moshtynsashit.' Boysie heaved with laughter until they got to Monaco, where he sat up and took another drink.

It was just after they had unfastened their seatbelts that Boysie had to make a dash to the shiny little lavatory at the tail end of the aircraft. His course was not particularly true, but, to the eternal relief of passengers in the aisle seats, he made it with half a second to spare. Fifteen minutes later he returned to his seat, still unsteady, having jettisoned all the brandy and his lunch. The lavatory's next occupant rang for the stewardess who threw several optical daggers in Boysie's direction as she marched tailwards firmly clutching a spraycan of air-freshener.

'Went a bit 'culiar. Musht'v been the lunch,' smiled Boysie, his eyes cross-focused on a point five inches to Iris's right.

But Iris stubbornly refused to speak; so, there being nothing else to do, Boysie went to sleep.

Dazed, with a tongue that seemed to have acquired a small mink jacket, and a head-ache which would have been a problem to a whole bottle of aspirin, Boysie weaved his way through the passport and customs for-malities: Iris clinging to his arm and aiming him in the general direction of the 'Arrivals' foyer. Through a kind of thick ectoplasm, he spotted Quadrant, who led them out to the opulent Lagonda Rapide.

'You don't look so hot, sport,' said Quad-rant as they drove off.

'Feel dreadful.'

'He got sloshed before we left.'

'Harry stinkers, eh? Naughty. Better sleep it off: got to be fit for the job. This is Peter, by the way.' He indicated the driver.

'Hi,' said Peter – a bull-like gentleman, whose broad back was surmounted by a dome of curved, wrinkled skin.

'Ho,' murmured Boysie, resting his head on the claret leather seat back, and drifting into sleep again.

'I hope he's all right,' said Iris. 'He's not the drinking kind.'

'We'll fix him up in Oxford.' Quadrant shifted in his seat, preparing to enjoy the ride.

'Yes. We'll give 'im one o' me specials in Oxford,' said Peter.

Martin – once more on duty as stake-out man at London Airport – winced at the tweak of rheumatic pain behind his right kneecap. He watched, puzzled, as the Lagonda pulled away from the 'Arrivals' exit. Turning his head, Martin nodded at the military-looking young man in the Zephyr parked strategically behind the blue BEA bus. The man lifted his arm in acknowledgment: the Zephyr drew out, overtook a taxi and settled comfortably on the Lagonda's tail.

The pain in Martin's knee had started earlier that afternoon; and, from long experience, he knew it to be a sign of trouble: his own built-in warning system, infallible as a finely adjusted computer. Martin was a plodder: a steady man, temperamentally unsuited to the extreme tensions of work in the field, but ideal for this kind of job. He liked nothing better than loitering with intent to observe – blessed, as he was, with an exceptional memory for faces, and an extraordinarily accurate nose (or knee) for trouble.

Martin had been a frustrated provincial newspaperman, his talents unrecognised, when the Organisation discovered him – nearly three years before. A smooth appeal – in the Mostyn manner – had been made to his sense of duty, and, within a few months, Martin was lost to the world – absorbed into that sea of Special Security men who spend their waking lives mingling with crowds on railway stations, or at air- and sea-ports: the public eyes; the Government-paid tipsters; Britain's secret police.

The knee started to twitch just after four o'clock. He was making his routine two hourly telephone report to Headquarters, when the operator cut in to announce that Number Two wanted words with him – urgently.

'Fly?' said Mostyn.

'Speaking.' Martin hoped that he wasn't going to get the 'buttons' gag again.

'Were you on duty on Saturday?'

'Yep.'

'Make the personal report to me? About "L" leaving the country?'

'That was me. Yes.'

'Good old Fly. Home is the hunter – watch out for him, will you?'

'It'll be a pleasure.'

'Not sure yet, but we think there's something fishy – positively cod-like. Reeks of skulduggery, but nothing definite to work on.'

The pain slid, like a white-hot needle, through Martin's knee. Instantly, as always, his senses reacted. The people moving in the foyer, outside the glass cubicle, were more sharply defined. He was increasingly aware of himself: of muscles and nerves and his place in the scheme of things.

'We hear,' Mostyn continued, 'that "L" and his young woman have changed their flight time. They're on the 105 from Nice. Be with you at 18.20. Watch, use your common and report to me – direct!'

'Right. His car's here, anyway. Left it in the park on Saturday. Noticed it when I came on duty this morning.'

'Fair enough. He'll probably drive straight back to town, but it might be safer to put a tail on him: see him off the premises and check which way he's heading. Anyone with you?'

'One of the juniors from the Training Centre. We'll set it up. I'll call you as soon as he gets under way.'

'Bully for you, Fly. Don't suppose there's anything in it, but it all makes good practice.'

Flight 105 touched down on the dot of

18.20. Martin, standing well-hidden behind a giggle of schoolgirls back from educational roving in Greece, watched Boysie and Iris come out of the Customs' Hall. 'L' looked tired and a bit bemused, thought Martin. Lucky beggar, he'd look tired himself after a couple of days in the South of France with Iris.

Then Boysie's expression changed. Peering across the foyer, he gave a barely perceptible nod and started off towards the exit. Martin looked in the direction of the nod. The man was leaning against a cigarette machine: thirtyish; sandy haired, with large, protruding ears. The man moved quickly behind Boysie and Iris, shepherding them out of the building. Within seconds they were in the Lagonda and away. It was more by luck than good planning that Duncan – Martin's trainee assistant, an ex-infantry captain – was able to get after them in the Zephyr.

Martin, concerned about this unexpected development, rapidly crossed into the entrance hall, bumped into a tall Texan buying himself a heap of life insurance from an automatic vendor, and catapulted into the only available telephone box – beating an Irish Roman Catholic priest by the length of a rosary, and causing the clerk to add the sin of uncharitable thoughts to his next confession list.

'Mostyn.' The voice crackled in his ear.

Martin shifted his position, placing himself so that Duncan could see him the moment he returned from chasing the Lagonda.

'Fly. He's arrived.'

'Welcome home, "L". Well?'

'As you say: fishy. Met by a slim man, about thirty-four; sandy hair; prominent ears; looks a bit effeminate. All drove away in a black Lagonda Rapide, licence XLK 9704. My boy's after them; be back any minute. Four altogether with the driver – a man, didn't get a look at him.'

'Recognise the bloke?'

'The one who met them?'

'Yes.'

'I've seen him somewhere. Picture in Records, I think. Rang a bell: I know the face but…'

'How did it feel?' Mostyn was a great one for intuition.

'Furtive. Unnatural. Not good.' He spotted Duncan coming across the foyer, his eyes searching the telephone boxes. Martin waved and opened the door:

'One minute, sir, here's my boy.' There was a quick, whispered conversation; then he turned back to the phone:

'They've gone left on the A4 – heading out of London.'

'Right. When's your relief due?'

'Half-an-hour.'

'Leave your lad in charge and get over here at a rate of knots. If "L's" friend isn't in the files, you'll have to do an Identikit. I want confirmed identification within the hour.'

'Right.'

Mostyn replaced the receiver and leaned back. To the tune of *West Side Story's* 'Maria' he began to sing softly:

'Big-Ears, he's just met a man with Big-Ears…'

Mostyn dialled Operations' Control:

'There's a possible flap concerning one of our operatives: code letter "L". Top secret. Nothing certain but I'll not leave the building until we've cleared it. I have two orders for you: Priority.'

'Shoot. I've got the tape running.' The Operations' Control Officer's voice was freezingly efficient.

'Primary. Black Lagonda Rapide, licence XLK 9740. Left London Airport five to ten minutes ago, heading west on the A4. I want a trace and general call. This car is not – repeat not – to be openly followed or intercepted. I want a distant cover with ten-minute reports as soon as contact is made. The occupants must not be alerted.'

'How many in the car?'

'Four. Three men and a girl.'

'We'll try and get a four-car interchangeable tail on them.' – A technique perfected by the Department whereby four cars continually shadowed a suspect vehicle: changing position every few miles; anticipating their quarry; covering every possible route ahead; never raising suspicion.

'Secondary. To Files and Records. I want a files' expert and an Identikit man standing by in Room Four. All Redland operatives – age-bracket, thirties: distinguishing marks: sandy hair, prominent ears.'

'Wilco.'

Mostyn's palms were damp. The first flea bites of concern, that had appeared on Saturday, were now spreading into a nettle-rash of anxiety.

At Slough, the Lagonda turned off the A4, cutting through to the A40. Boysie was still sleeping it off, while Iris dozed, the fingers of her right hand resting on Boysie's sleeve in an almost protective gesture.

'I think we're all right,' said Quadrant. 'Forget about the round-the-houses route. We'll go direct and dawdle after we leave Oxford.'

'You're the boss,' said Peter.

Quadrant glanced into the back seat: 'I wish I was,' he muttered.

'That's him,' said Martin.

'You won't need me then,' said the Identikit man who had a date.

'You're sure?' From Mostyn.

'As eggs.'

'Good show.'

They were seated round a bare table under the shadowless glare of a naked light bulb hanging low from the ceiling. The Identikit man nodded and quietly left the room. The filing expert was looking at the photograph.

'Well?' said Mostyn.

'You're absolutely certain about this?' said the expert.

'That's the man. No doubt at all.'

'Come on then. Give.' Mostyn sounded over-anxious.

The expert, a tall, aquiline Scot, bent from his chair and selected a thick, buff card folder from the stack piled at his feet:

'Nasty,' he said. 'Very nasty. We're in trouble, Colonel Mostyn. Real name Constantine Alexei Skabichev. A braw laddie. Parents supposed to be White Russian immigrants: arrived here 1916. Naturalised 1925. The old man made a packet out of scrap: nothing but the best for wee Connie. Born 1926, May 10th. Educated Eton and Wadham: probably conditioned from the day of his birth. We didn't cotton on to them until 1956 when Connie went to Switzerland on holiday and was spotted by one of our people in Russia – hundred to one shot. Somehow the parents got out of the country before we could net them; and, as far as we know, this is Connie's first return visit since '56 – suppose he got in through Ireland.'

'What's his speciality act?' asked Mostyn.

'He's reckoned as one of the brightest all-round boys of the KGB. Ruthless; a fixer; natural trouble-maker. Assisted in three defections. Spends a lot of time in East Berlin. Incidentally, he was present at the Greville Wynn trial last month. We know Vassall met him in Moscow. Let's see? Oh yes ... they tried to palm him off as interpreter to one of the cultural missions recently – last year sometime; but we kicked up and the FO got them to withdraw the lad. To be quite honest with you, sir, it must be something pretty big bringing him here.' He picked up the photograph:

'Surprised he's never tried plastic surgery on those ears.'

The telephone burped. Mostyn took it:

'Mostyn.'

'The Lagonda's turned on to the A40: heading towards Oxford.'

'Thank you. Keep me posted.' He replaced the receiver. 'They're heading for Oxford.'

'Are we going to pick them up?'

'No, leave it a while. We've got tabs on them for the time being. Let's see what develops, I'd like to know what they're doing with "L".'

Back in his own office, Mostyn poured

himself a large whisky and began to make a logical appraisal of the situation. Boysie had always been a liability, but under no circumstances could one imagine 'L' as a target for defection overtures – for machine guns, bombs, falls from high buildings, yes: but not defection: that could be ruled out altogether.

On Saturday, Boysie had left, suddenly, for Nice, with Iris. He was breaking regulations, but there was nothing sinister about that. He had, himself, dwelt with great pleasure on thoughts of a weekend with Iris. Then, on Saturday evening, Boysie had disappeared, in Menton, for a matter of nearly six hours. Blueboy had reported an unidentified male visitor on Sunday. That could have been Skabichev (he made a mental note to do something about Blueboy: the fellow hadn't even sent a description). Tonight 'L' had returned to England, a day earlier than intended, and was now on the way to Oxford, with Skabichev.

The opposition were taking risks, which inevitably meant that something big was in the air. As far as he could see, there were three possibilities. Boysie had either been drugged, hypnotised or conned into performing some kind of duty for the other side. If one followed the argument to its ultimate length, there was only one answer. Boysie was back to kill – it was his only talent. Somehow, a kill had been fixed by the opposition. But with what object? And who was the target?

They arrived in Oxford at nine o'clock and dined at the Mitre, among sombre clerics and retiring gentlewomen in not so reduced circumstances. Boysie was beginning to feel his old self again. From the Mitre they wandered over to the Randolph and sat sipping occasional gins in the Star Bar until ten thirty. At ten forty-five they were on the road again, driving very slowly.

At midnight, Mostyn's telephone rang for the tenth time.

'They've just passed through Stratford-on-Avon.' Mostyn looked at the Security diary and frowned:

'Thank you. I'm coming down.'

A special map had been set up on a tilted drawing board in a corner of the Operations' Control Room – a series of flags tracing the Lagonda from London to the borders of Warwickshire. Mostyn stood looking at it: trying to make up his mind. They were in the Midlands now. His instinct told him exactly who the target was. His common sense said it was impossible. At last he decided. They would have to be brought in: now, before it was too late. He was about to speak, when the Operations'

Officer came over:

'They've lost contact.'

'Damn!' said Mostyn. 'Where?'

'Somewhere on the Warwick road, the other side of Stratford. Just disappeared into the night.'

Now he would have to rely solely on his instinct. If he was wrong...

'If they make contact again, let me know at once. Get on to Records. I want everything we've got on RAF Gayborough.'

At quarter-past midnight, the Lagonda turned into a side road and drove on to the grass verge. Peter switched off the lights.

'Sackfuls of time, kiddies,' said Quadrant. 'Have a bit of shut-eye here, then we'll get the lad kitted out.'

'Not tired now,' said Boysie.

'You will be by eleven o'clock tomorrow, sport. Take it while you can.'

'What the bloody hell d'you mean – they've gone?' Mostyn was livid. For the third time, the pale and bewildered filing clerk tried to explain:

'The Gayborough folder's there, sir, but it's empty.'

This was the first piece of substantial evidence. Mostyn's intuition was leading him in the right direction:

'Who's got the duplicates? Air Ministry?'

'Yes, sir.'

'That settles it.' To the Operations' Officer: 'I want a full enquiry when this thing's over. Get on to Air Ministry. I want everything they've got; have it ready for me to pick up in twenty minutes. Lay on a car and driver for me. Is that Fly bloke still in the building?'

'Martin? Yes, said he felt like sticking around.'

'Martin? That his name? Tell him to report to me, we're going for a ride. Then get a call through to the Commanding Officer, RAF Gayborough – drag him out of bed if you've got to. When I've finished with him I want a priority to Security at Buck House. Got it. Red Emergency.'

'You look gorgeous, darling.' Iris was grinning as Boysie rubbed the foul matt-black make-up under his chin.

They had pulled down the car's blinds, and switched on the light so that Boysie could see to get the camouflage smock over his head. He looked at himself in the hand mirror that Iris was holding up for him.

'Bloody chocolate coloured coon.'

'Why did de chicken cross de road?' said Quadrant.

'Very humorous,' said Boysie without any enthusiasm.

'Just load the magazine and fill a couple of spare clips for yourself, will you, sport?'

Quadrant passed a Lee Enfield magazine, two cartridge clips and a box of blanks into the back of the car: 'Safety and all that.'

Boysie pushed five blanks into the magazine, pressing down with the ball of his thumb to make sure the spring was working easily. He then filled the two clips.

'Let's have the magazine and I'll load this dangerous thing for you,' said Quadrant, bending down and sliding the rifle from its hiding place under the seat.

Boysie handed him the magazine. Quadrant dropped it noiselessly in his lap, his hand slipping into his jacket pocket, stealing out with a duplicate. He glanced down. The substitute held five long pointed cupro-nickel rounds of live .303 ammunition. Quadrant snapped it into place in front of the trigger-guard. There was a metallic clack-clack as he pulled on the bolt arm and loaded the weapon.

'There we are, sport. There's one up the spout and the safety-catch is on. No need for you to touch it again until morning. You don't want to be fiddling around with the bolt when you're up there – noise carries the hell of a way.'

He opened the car door: 'Now, if the lovely Iris will change places with me, I'll come and sit by our hero so that we can go over the final stages of the exercise – just for luck.'

'You don't flippin' trust my memory, do you?' said Boysie.

Quadrant flashed his most urbane smile: 'Frankly, no,' he said.

'Mostyn and Martin,' said Mostyn. 'Sounds like a double act, old boy, doesn't it?'

'Or a firm of dubious solicitors,' replied Martin.

Under the shaded light in the back of the car, they were examining the maps and photographs of RAF Gayborough: speeding along the M1.

'It's all a bit cloak and dagger though isn't it?' From Martin.

'It's the only theory that fits. Can you figure out any other reason for side-tracking our laddie and whipping him off to this part of the country?'

'No, but it seems a bit way out.'

'At this point in the game we'll have to assume that they are way out: that they've persuaded him to do the kill. Why? That's the question. As far as I can see, if we're right...'

'If you're right...'

'Don't quibble. If I'm right, their operation has two objects. One, to assassinate a member of the royal family. Two, to drop the Department right in the clag.' Against his judgment, Mostyn had been forced to reveal Boysie's true role with the Department – a decision which worried him: the fewer people who knew about 'L' the better.

He went on: 'If they are trying to put the mockers on us, then the kill has got to be pretty obvious. He's either going to do the Duke's car on the way to Gayborough, or he'll have a go at him on the spot; and the most likely place seems to be here – when he inspects the guard of honour at the main gate. What would you do if you wanted to have a crack at him, and get caught at the same time?'

Martin picked up the aerial photograph: 'Pop him in that clump of trees with a noisy machine gun, or a very loud rifle.'

'Quite,' said Mostyn. 'And that's where we're going to look for him. If he hasn't turned up by first light, then we'll have to cancel the Duke's visit and put out a general call for the whole bang shooting match of them. And if that happens, then God help friend Boysie...'

'The Bloody Tower?'

'No less, Martin, old fruit. Sedition and privy conspiracy: sedition and privy...' He tailed off. For the next ten minutes Mostyn sat in a box of private worry: his mind churning and considering the unpleasant permutations of punishment should his undoubted culpability in the Boysie saga ever get into the daily Press.

Boysie watched the Lagonda's tail-lights disappear into the thin three-in-the-morning light, the taste of Iris's farewell lipstick still rosy in his saliva. It was a mild night – clear with high white streaks percursing dawn. He glanced down at the luminous dial of his watch: ten-past-three. Below his feet, on the road's verge, there seemed to be a slight scattering of snow. Hawthorn: he could smell it – the sickly odour of summer Sundays and walks with the village girls.

Boysie turned, hitched the rifle sling on to his shoulder and stalked through the gap in the hedge: aiming towards the skyline point which Quadrant had given him as a bearing. After the last few hours it felt strange to be alone in the quiet before sunrise: something like a parachutist, dropped from the oily roar of engines and fabric into the silence of empty air. Boysie's guts rattled at the thought of leaping – with or without a parachute – from an aeroplane: the idea of falling was another of his phobias. This was damn silly, he thought: three in the morning and traipsing across a stretch of countryside to play schoolboy games. But it was just the kind of thing you expected from a nit like Mostyn. He was probably down there now, tucked up in an officers' mess bed over the horizon, dreaming sadistic dreams about Boysie blundering about the countryside, splashing through platters of cowpats and wrenching his ankles in rabbit holes.

The grass rustled, dew-damp under his feet. Boysie sniffed the air – a mixture of wet, growing grass and freshly cut meadows: the smell of cricket pitches and Whit Monday Sports Day at the Grammar. He plodded, excelsior-like, onwards and upwards, occasionally shifting the weight of the rifle on to his other shoulder, and thinking of long ago when the country was an open book beneath a pair of muddy boots.

Finally, he reached the top of the rise, dropping to his knees, so that he would not be outlined against the grey gleam of sky. Below, RAF Gayborough sprawled into the murky distance: the airfield to his left, long crossed pencils of runway dotted with shielded yellow oblongs. For the past ten minutes Boysie had been conscious of the whine of jets; now, suddenly, they were released in a great eardrumming roar. He could see the red and green flashing lights alternating and moving fast along the runway; and the huge dark triangle of a V-Bomber came hurtling off the concrete, growing bigger and bigger. The noise seemed to surround him, as though the machine was bent on singling him out and smashing itself straight into his stomach. Automatically, Boysie pushed himself flat into the grass as it nosed, harmless and high, away to his left: the ground shaking under the reverberating crack of its boosters.

This small episode brought on one of his nervous attacks. Up to now, apart from his silent insults directed towards Mostyn's person, Boysie had been relatively unflurried, tasting the freshness of the country air and dreaming of his boyhood. But the noise of this beast-plane had touched off the raw spots on the tips of his nerves.

The clump of trees was clearly discernible, a little to the right, downhill. Now, wholly disenchanted, Boysie descended, ears cocked for alien noises, his heart clocking up a more than average rate, and that well-known nasty abdominal sinking feeling.

There were four trees – elms – set in a rough square bounded by bushy under-growth; between them, the ground sloped into a narrow saucer. Boysie sat down in the centre, put the rifle at his feet and stretched. It was quite light now, almost four o'clock, and Boysie felt distinctly uneasy: as though he was not alone. Slowly he turned, shoot-ing quick little glances into the bushes, and above to the thick branches which formed an arch of heavy leaves over his head.

Remembering the object of the exercise, he picked up the rifle, climbed to the rim of the saucer and began to search around for a good firing point. A slight, natural fold in the ground lay directly behind a small gap in the bushes; through it he could see the road and a clear arc which covered the main gate and its surround. Dropping into the prone position, Boysie squirmed about until he was comfortable. There was plenty of cover and the rifle rested easily on a clod of earth in front of him. He pushed the butt hard into his shoulder and squinted down the telescopic lens, traversing the whole of the main gate and guard room, his right forefinger curled round the safety inactive trigger. A service policeman was wandering to and fro, on lonely duty outside the guard room. Boysie adjusted the sights and brought the centre of the crossed wires dead into position on the policeman's icecream white cap.

'Puttew!' He made the mouth noise of gunfire which came thrusting back from the cowboy and Indian days. A noise in the trees startled him, almost making him drop the rifle and look up. But it was only the mewing of baby owls, nestling somewhere among the foliage, waiting for mama to return with a morsel of mouse for breakfast.

Boysie put down the rifle and slid back into the centre of the saucer. He looked at his watch. Seven bleeding hours up here alone, he thought venomously. Well, at least he could have a crafty cigarette while he inflicted some mental agonies on his boss. He fumbled in the camouflage smock for his smoking equipment, lit a king-size filter and blew a modestly symmetrical smoke ring.

He did not hear the slight movement in the bushes behind him. A moment later, he was face down and struggling hard: a pair of arms wrapped round his legs and a lump of flesh-filled sleeve clamped over his mouth. The first reaction was that he had been spotted – it was the end of the exercise. But these boys were playing it rough. Through the mouth-stopping sleeve he was mumbling:

'All right! Coronet ... bugger you, all right... CO ... RO ... NET.'

The sleeve relaxed:

'Stop it, you half-baked, wall-eyed bastard!' said Boysie.

'That's no way to talk to your superiors, Boysie, old Boysie,' cooed Mostyn.

Heaving and fighting for breath, Boysie twisted round to face the Second-in-Command:

'I might have bloody known...' He was shivering all over from the sudden shock: '...you ... and ... your ... bloody Coronet. Well, that's it ... I've bloody had it... You can take your coronet and stuff it ... velvet ... ermine and all.'

'What coronet, Boysie? Or should I say whose coronet?' Mostyn had got to his feet and was looking down at Boysie whose legs were held fast by a dishevelled Martin:

'Come on, old lad, this isn't a TV soap

opera: we can't wait for next week's instalment. I'm not a mind reader, you know. I want to hear all about coronet.' Mostyn squatted on to his haunches: his face only a few inches from Boysie: 'If you don't tell me, laddie, and quickly, I'll see you're done good and proper. You won't know whether you're on your arse or Easter Day for the next ninety-nine years – and some!'

Boysie gave an anguished cry, not unlike that of a young bullock in extreme pain. He recognised the ground glass tone in Mostyn's voice and knew that, somehow, he had come, as they say, a real purler.

9 – *ENGLAND*

Tuesday June 11th 1963

VULTURE

They were still among the trees: Boysie staring incredulously at the five rounds of live .303 ammunition that Martin had quietly ejected from the rifle. Mostyn held the golden quintet of death in the hollow of his palm, and thrust the hand under Boysie's nose:

'You're useless, old Oakes. Abso-bloody-lutely useless.'

'I know.' Boysie, swathed in shock and misery had touched bedrock: shaking his head from side to side, numbed like a man who had just been informed of the sudden extermination of his entire family.

He had told his story, halting and uncertain, between bouts of Mostyn's most cutting sarcasm. Now, he was a man drained of any dignity. The end, he knew, was inevitable. The job was finished, and it would only be a matter of time before the whole truth came spouting into the open:

'There's something else I ought to say…'

he began, plucking up courage, trying to end things quickly: a kind of hara-kiri.

'Not now, laddie.' Mostyn looked at him, his face softening. 'Boysie, you're an oaf. Still, I suppose it could have happened to any of us.'

The three men were silent: Martin, looking embarrassed, fiddling with the bolt arm of the rifle; Boysie, his face turned up towards Mostyn, like a big, daft spaniel trying to regain favour. But, underneath the look, Mostyn's switch to sympathy had served only to reignite Boysie's inherent dislike of the man. He resented the Second-in-Command's compassion, as the proud poor resent charity.

'You realise what's happened, I suppose?' Mostyn asked. Then, not waiting for Boysie's reply, he continued: 'It isn't just the Duke they are after, you know. You'd have shot him, cold as mutton, with that damn rifle; and you'd have been topped for it. But, long before they took you on the nine o'clock walk, there would have been hints in the newspapers: little bits of tittle-tattle: gossip. Information would have fallen into people's hands. There would have been talk. Members asking awkward questions in the House. Your name would have been linked with the Department, and, no matter how much we denied and wriggled, there would have been a public enquiry. They were after *us*, old boy.'

Boysie nodded painfully:

'What do we do now?'

'That, me old thing, is what I'm trying to decide. I suppose we'd better put out a general call for your friends. I didn't really want the Special Branch brought into it, but I don't see any other way. We're particularly interested in Quadrant...'

'So am I...'

'...His real name's Skabichev, by the way. You know, I have a feeling that we ought to play this one to the limit. They're bound to have someone watching at eleven o'clock. If we cordon the area we'll stand a good chance of nabbin' him. Something tells me that we should see it through.'

'You mean brief the Duke and let Boysie take a couple of shots at him – blanks? Do it their way?' asked Martin.

'Not Boysie. I'm not leaving him up here.' Mostyn's brow was incised with puzzled wrinkles: 'There's something missing. Something I've forgotten. A piece not in place. There's more to it than the Duke.'

He turned his back on the others and climbed up to Boysie's firing point. For about five minutes he lay, looking down on the brightening camp. At last, with a decisive movement, he raised himself from the ground, slid down the bank, and faced Boysie and Martin:

'How's this then?' It wasn't a question. The plan was already fully conceived: nothing they said, or did, would change his mind now. His voice was steady as a count-down: 'Boysie and I go and get things moving straight away – Police, RAF Regiment, Special Branch. The area will be cordoned off within the hour. Maybe we'll even have them in a bag.' He paused, a quick smile switched on and off like a neon sign. 'In case we don't, I'll get on to the Duke: give him the full strength, and tell him what to do. He'd better stay in the car when it arrives at the main gate. It'll save his dignity if he doesn't have to roll around playing dead.' He pointed at Martin: 'You stay up here with the rifle. As soon as they open the car door, you give 'em five rounds rapid. The boys'll be briefed to make a fuss – slam the door, drive quickly through the gate, bit of panic, you know the kind of thing. Anyone watching's going to think they've pulled it off – they won't try anything else on the Duke anyway. If there is a secondary stage to the plan, they'll probably go ahead and put it into operation.' He paused, trying to measure their reactions: 'Boysie? We'll be up in the control tower. From there we can see the whole camp and airfield: be ready for any emergency: and if anything does happen, then we'll have to play it by ear. You game, Martin?'

'Anything you say.' Martin's knee was jabbing out its warning pain signals at quick, regular intervals.

'Right. Boysie, we'll have to risk going down in full view – they may have someone watching us already. We've got no option though.'

'Honestly, I don't really see why we have to go through all this palaver.' Boysie was still ready to throw in his hand.

'Neither do I, old boy. But then, for nine-tenths of the time, I work on intuition. Give those blanks to Martin and we'll get going.'

To Martin he said:

'We'll let you know if we catch 'em before the balloon goes up.'

They descended to the road: Boysie, woebegone in his black-face make-up, trudging behind Mostyn. Martin thought to himself that they looked unusually like master and slave.

Ten thirty. Boysie, clean and in a borrowed RAF-blue sweater and slacks, was looking out from the control tower, across the airfield. A Valiant was coming in over the boundaries to his right; its undercarriage down, flaps and dive brakes extended. It seemed to be moving in slow motion, as though suspended by an invisible, unbreakable, wire. The aircraft touched down – puffs of smoke from the tyres: a quivering growl as the jets were reversed.

'Metro Oscar Three Two Five. Clear taxi to dispersal. Closing down on your frequency.' The young Flight Lieutenant had a brown, dispassionate voice. From the small, round speaker, angled into the control panel in front of him, came the disembodied voice of the Valiant's co-pilot:

'Metro Oscar Three Two Five. Roger and out. Thank you.'

The Flight Lieutenant turned to the chief controller, a stocky Wing Commander, hot in his best blue and medals, all preened for the royal visit.

'That's it, sir. Pattern's clear,' said the Flight Lieutenant.

The control tower staff relaxed slightly, except for the two WRAF Radar officers, immobile, their eyes following the scanners. The Wing Commander went over to the door that opened, from the long bowed glass surround, on to the balcony which ran round the squat building. Outside, Mostyn stood talking with the Group Captain – a craggy Highlander, more clan chieftain than Station Commander: known to everyone, behind his back, as Black Angus.

'Holding pattern's clear, sir. We're closed until the special demonstration,' reported the Wing Commander.

'Guid. Thank ye.' The Groupie led Mostyn back into the greenhouse of the control tower. For a second, Boysie's concentration was disturbed by a tall helpless-looking WRAF, who had momentarily raised her head from the swinging circle of light on her scanner. A pair of smoky-grey eyes locked with his across the room. Boysie swallowed hard at that old, old feeling, and quickly turned his attention back to Mostyn and Black Angus, who were bearing down on him.

'Oakes and yerself would be best placed inside. Somewhere over here.' The Group Captain indicated the left-hand side of the glass sweep. 'Ye get a grand view of the station from here – main gate, and that high ground yer so interested in. And I hope, Mr Oakes,' he prodded at Boysie's chest with a bony finger, 'that ye haven't any stones on ye. Ye know what they say about people in glass houses.' His laugh came grumbling from the back of his throat. The control tower staff tittered politely. It was the Groupie's favourite joke about the tower. Boysie opened his mouth to reply. but Mostyn recognised the look of innocent humour.

'Boysie!' He sounded like a man calling a hound to heel. Boysie obeyed, joining Mostyn by the window, fingering the field glasses that hung from a leather strap round his neck. He looked towards the main gate, sensing the Groupie behind them, breathing hard. A staff car was drawing up in front of the guard room. He lifted the glasses. A shining service policeman was leaning forward, talking to whoever was in the rear of the car. The driver was a WRAF. She had something of Iris about her, he thought. Boysie felt a small pang of concern for the copper-haired girl he had left to the mercy of Quadrant. What had they done with her? Mostyn had said not to worry, but the Lagonda had been found abandoned four miles from the village of Gayborough: no trace of its occupants. Boysie jumped as Black Angus snapped behind him:

'Check with the main gate, please. Who's that coming in?'

The Wing Commander picked up a telephone. A moment later:

'The party from Group, sir. They've gone to the Mess.'

'Aye, they would.'

Boysie once more put the glasses to his eyes, focusing on the clump of trees. He could just make out Martin's face peeping from between the bushes. Mostyn was scanning the skyline. Pretending to be a bloody U-Boat Commander, thought Boysie.

The control tower staff were growing restless. Tension was beginning to press in with the sun, now high and warm. Down by the main gate, the Guard of Honour was falling in: razor-pressed and balanced,

236

conscious that royalty was imminent. On the far side of the airfield, there was some activity around the dispersal points. The electric clock impassively nudged away the seconds. Ten forty-five. Ten fifty-five.

Boysie lowered the field glasses and glanced towards the main gate. Another staff car was turning in. The telephone shrilled by the Wing Commander's elbow:

'Sir!' There was alarm in the senior controller's voice. 'Another lot; say they're from Group.'

'Do they now? Hold 'em,' said the Groupie. Then: 'That canna be right, Mostyn, there's only one party coming from Group. Sound like customers for you...'

'Definitely from Group, sir.' The Wing Commander looked desperate. 'Perkins recognises Wing Commander Reardon.'

'What about the other lot then? Ring the mess...'

'Sir?' Concern from the Flight Lieutenant: 'Flavell's starting up the Vulture without clearance. There's ten minutes to go before he's scheduled...' The rising howl of a jet engine could be heard to the right of the field. Boysie craned forward. He could see the slim snout of an aircraft's nose protruding from a screen of small buildings quarter of a mile away, just off the perimeter track which circled the field.

'Find out what the blue hades young

Flavell's playing at.'

The Flight Lieutenant began the patter:

'Control to One Four Five Echo. You are not clear to start engines...'

Mostyn looked stricken:

'You've got the Vulture here?'

'Aye. Didn't ye ken? Did nobody tell ye? She's over there, see.' Black Angus pointed towards the buildings.

'No, by God, I didn't ken...' Mostyn stopped. That was it. He had known. It was in the Top Secret release he had read last Saturday. This was the missing piece. The Vulture.

'Can't raise Flavell, sir,' from the Flight Lieutenant. The Wing Commander had been stabbing at the telephone dial:

'Can't raise the ground crew either, sir.'

The Group Captain was still talking to Mostyn:

'Aye. Flavell, the test pilot, flew her down from Farnborough last night with his crew of operators. They're demonstrating it for the Duke...' Light seemed to dawn: 'Man, you don't think...?'

Boysie was quite lost. He could see that Mostyn was clicking like a Geiger counter deep in the heart of a nuclear reactor. Mostyn all but screamed:

'Anyone got a fast car?'

The Wing Commander took a single step towards him:

'MG. Down there. Red.'

'The keys. Quick man, the keys. Boysie, with me. Stop that bloody aeroplane!' He snatched the keys from the Wing Commander and flung himself at the balcony door, racing round to the rear of the building. A .38 service revolver half out of his hip pocket. Boysie, still a shade hazy, was after him. Black Angus, beetroot-faced, was yelling:

'Have ye gone mad, man? The Duke's car... Mostyn, ye fool!'

'Vulture's got both engines going, sir.' The Wing Commander had unbuttoned his jacket. The control tower felt like a time bomb.

'I think she's taxying...' The Flight Lieutenant looked pale.

Both Mostyn and Boysie heard the five, quick, distant pops floating from the direction of the main gate. They had just reached the iron steps which spiralled, like a fire escape, from the balcony: Mostyn turned his head and shouted back:

'The Duke's arrived! That's Martin!'

The MG, crimson and raffish, was parked on a hard-standing behind the tower. Mostyn vaulted over the door and had the engine running, seconds before Boysie tumbled headlong into the passenger seat. The gears clashed. Mostyn wrenched at the wheel, and they bumped off the concrete:

the tyres howling as the little car skidded on to the perimeter track. Mostyn banged her into top and flicked the .38 revolver into Boysie's lap:

'You'll need that,' he yelled above the whine of wind and engine.

'What's it all about. I'm not with it,' mouthed Boysie.

Mostyn pointed along the bonnet:

'The Vulture.'

The aircraft was taxying fast, turning towards the far end of the field, a good half-mile in front of them – a vicious-looking piece of aircraft design. Trident antennae reached forward, like a snake's tongue, from a slim silver nose which curved down to form a long bulbous fuselage. Aft of the wings – steeply angled and tapering to a startling point – the fuselage swept upwards, pencilling out to a V-shaped tail, under which Boysie could see two cheroot-like jet-pods. The machine seemed to lean forward, very near to the ground, with undercarriage legs sprouting from the lowest points of nose and fuselage. It had about it a savage look. As though the designers had spent their lives studying grotesque prehistoric flying reptiles, and then sought to translate them into terms of metal and fabric.

'What is it?'

'Flying test bed for the M31... Search and destroy anti-missile equipment. You don't read your security handouts.' Even at a time like this, Mostyn was ready with a gibe. But Boysie knew all about the M31. No one in the Department was ever allowed to forget about it. The M31 was the hottest security problem since the H-Bomb. A flying death ray for missiles, with a range of over 500 miles. It could seek and explode an enemy rocket within three minutes of launching. As yet it was unperfected but the boffins reckoned that within three years, five specially-designed aircraft carrying the phenomenally expensive M31 could neutralise the West against any nuclear attack.

As they shot past the Vulture's dispersal area, Boysie glimpsed at least three bodies – one in grey flying overalls – spread across the tarmac.

'Must have got through in that first staff car,' shouted Mostyn: '…Your friends… The Duke's only a diversion… Hold on!'

They were gaining on the Vulture, Mostyn swinging the car out to the right, approaching from the beam, well clear of the high tail jets which they could now hear screeching over the MG's engine. As the side of the aircraft came into view, Boysie could see an oblong hatch, open, low down in the fuselage and only about six feet from the ground. A figure seemed to be spread-eagled across it, trying to pull a door into place. The Vulture had left the perimeter

241

track, turning and selecting the main runway which cut down the centre of the airfield.

They were closing rapidly now, moving in a wide circle, bouncing over the grass which lined the edges of the runway. To Boysie, nothing seemed to be stable: the landscape, the Vulture, the ground, all juddering and quaking as the car rattled forward. The figure in the hatch looked up, spotting them: his ears appeared to be shaking in time to the jets. It was Quadrant.

Mostyn had his foot pushed right down on to the floorboards, and seemed intent on ramming the aircraft. Boysie could not believe this was happening. He clung to his seat, buffeting and jolting: horrified at the speed and noise. Through a pumping blur he saw Quadrant's hand come up, and heard Mostyn shriek:

'Get him, Boysie, for Chrissake…!'

Suddenly, in the urgency of the moment, he found callousness: breaking through the fear barrier. Boysie's hatred towards Quadrant turned to action: jabbing his arm forward with the gun; closing his left eye to take aim. But, before he could squeeze the trigger, there were three tiny flashes from the hatchway. Boysie heard a crack above his head. There was a jar and splutter as the windscreen shattered. The car slewed off course, and he heard Mostyn give a quick, painful intake of breath.

The car righted itself, and Boysie lifted his arm again. Unsteady in the rocking seat, he aimed for the legs and fired twice: the hatch growing bigger as they streaked towards the Vulture. Quadrant made a grab at his knees, which seemed to crumble under him. Mouth open in terror, hands clawing at the air, Quadrant pitched forward through the hatch and on to the concrete in front of the car's singing wheels.

Mostyn could do nothing about it. They lurched upwards as the body hit their front bumper. The car tilted precariously then rolled back and they were racing on again; closer and closer to the fuselage and the hatchway. Boysie could hear the jets, above their heads, accelerating to a high-pitched whistle. He glanced at Mostyn who was crouched over the wheel, blood soaking his shirt where the bullet had smashed into his left shoulder.

'Can't go on much longer,' Mostyn shouted. 'Jump for the hatch ... got to stop ... take-off...'

Boysie curled himself onto the passenger seat, hanging on to the door, his eyes fastened to the dark slit almost above his head.

'Jump!' yelled Mostyn.

He reached up with his hands and, pushing with his feet, projected himself through the opening, landing inside the aircraft –

243

legs and buttocks still waving through the hatch; the breath forced from his lungs by the sudden jolt. As he hit the floor, so the Vulture seemed to thrust forward, leaving the MG behind, like a spent runner.

Boysie dragged himself through the hatch and swung into a sitting position: eyes misty, heart drumming and breathing reduced to great fish-like gulps. He tried to relax: concentrating on controlling his body, but the shock reaction of fear crept over him in a rippling tremor. Hauling himself to his feet, he realised that the floor of the fuselage seemed to be raked upwards. He stumbled to the side of the hatch, intending to look out in search of Mostyn and the MG. Below him, the ground was sliding away: miniature buildings, fields and trees steadily moving farther off. The Vulture was airborne. Boysie shrank back from the open hatch and, true to form, was horribly sick.

A minute later, he wiped his mouth with the back of his hand, startled to find that he was still clutching the revolver. The fuselage ran forward between two complex lanes of what looked like radar equipment: long panels of instruments, with four hooded scanners. The priceless M31. Boysie edged past the maze of apparatus, up to the forward bulkhead and the small, grey door which, he knew, must lead on to the flight deck.

The fear was still with him, but the trembling had stopped. Slowly his mind began to accept the situation. Nothing seemed to matter except getting on to the flight deck and forcing whoever was flying the machine to turn back. Perhaps, he thought, this might possibly make up for the past deceptions. He turned the handle and pulled. The door swung back and Boysie stepped on to the flight deck, levelling the revolver towards the pilot's seat. Things had become so dangerous in the last few minutes that he was past caring.

'All right. The party's over,' he shouted, realising that it was a bit on the melodramatic side.

The Co-ordinator, cool at the controls, twisted round. Boysie stopped short, his eyes wide, the revolver dangling in his hand. The Co-ordinator was silent for a moment, regaining poise after the shock of Boysie's entrance. Then:

'It would be you, Boysie. I *thought* something had gone wrong. You stupid bastard.' Iris contemptuously turned her back on him and concentrated on swinging the Vulture in a wide climbing turn towards the sun.

10 – *ENGLAND*

Tuesday June 11th 1963

CO-ORDINATOR

The silence was eerie on the flight deck. With the engines far away in the tail, noise was reduced to a barely audible whistle: the sound of a vacuum cleaner in the semi-detached next door. They hardly seemed to be moving, and, except for the slight tremor under his feet, Boysie thought, they might well be still on the ground. It did not do for him to think too deeply about what lay beneath his feet: the stretch of air and open sky.

Boysie shifted slightly, leaning back against the door, trying to adjust his mind to the fact that Iris was flying the Vulture. That Iris, pride of his bed, was on the other side. An enemy. When he spoke, his voice was dry, throaty with nervousness:

'Sorry, Iris, you'll have to turn her round. I've got a gun on you...'

Iris dropped her hand on to the control pedestal and moved the throttles forward a fraction. Without turning, she said:

247

'Boysie, you'll find a dial on the door – like a safe mechanism. Close the door and turn the dial fully clockwise, would you.'

Boysie did not move.

'Quickly, Boysie. We're climbing. I want to pressurise the flight deck; if I don't, we'll both be unconscious in a very few minutes and that's not going to help either of us.'

Boysie obeyed. This is ridiculous, he thought. It can't be happening. I'm in bed, with Iris. It's a scorching nightmare.

'Iris, if you don't turn back, I'll...' An angry parent to a reluctant infant.

'You'll do what? Shoot me? I don't think so, darling.'

Boysie climbed forward, sliding himself into the co-pilot's seat, the gun still pointing at the girl. Her WRAF uniform skirt was hoisted well up her thighs: the long, gorgeous legs stretched elegantly down to stockinged feet pressed firmly on the rudder pedals. She had removed her jacket, which hung behind the seat, and Boysie noted the thick, irregular stain of sweat spreading under the armpits of her shirt. He was conscious of his own body, wet with fright.

'No, I don't think you'll shoot me, Boysie,' she said. She might have been in a bedroom daring him into rape. There was something remarkably sexy about the situation.

'I know you as well as you know yourself.' She was smiling, concentrating on the controls as she spoke. 'You detest flying. You need me, darling; and you'll just have to go where I'm going. There's no one else to fly it.'

Boysie played what he thought was his trump card:

'It doesn't matter all that much. After what your lot has done to me, I've had it with the Department anyway. The RAF'll catch up with you soon enough; then you'll be forced to go down. You haven't got an earthly, Iris.'

'No? They'll have to find us first.'

'Every tracking station in...'

'Nuts to the tracking stations. We've got a head start. Know what this is?' She pointed to a small, square, black box, attached, with rubber suckers, to the windscreen. It looked like a cheap transistor radio.

'The latest thing, darling. A radar dazzler. Confuses the beams and puts the radio out of joint. Trouble is our people haven't got it wholly effective yet. Still, it'll work for another twenty minutes: and that's quite a time at this speed. Anyway, they're not likely to use fighters – except as a last resort. This baby's rather precious.' She paused. The aircraft rocked under them. 'We've been planning this for quite a long time, you know: thought of practically everything.'

'But how the...' Boysie was balanced between terror and curiosity.

'How the hell did I get mixed up with Redland?' They were nosing into cloud now: a rash of dew settling over the windscreen. Iris shot him a quick pouting glance:

'The Department's terribly naïve, you know,' she said. 'When I joined, they screened me in every possible direction. Checked everything, even my sex life which, at that time, Boysie, was beyond reproach. They dug and dug like the seven little dwarfs, and came up with all the answers. They only missed one thing: the fact that when I was seventeen – two years before I became a junior in the Department typing pool – I was an active member of the International Youth Council. That was in '55, and I was terribly proud, because the IYC selected me as a representative to a conference in Prague. And that's where I was recruited.'

'You mean ... ever since you joined the Department, you've been working for...'

'They got me the job, darling. Every single leave I've had has been spent, ostensibly, in Switzerland. But no one bothered to check that. In fact, I've been elsewhere doing a spot of adult education. Last year they made me Co-ordinator of an action group. We had a special mission – to get this thing. You've no idea, Boysie, the organisation's terrific. Do you know, I spent the whole of my last leave learning to fly big jets. I'm rather good

250

at it, don't you think?'

Boysie had always imagined his situation with the Department was fringed with fantasy, but this prattling luscious doll... It was pure burlesque:

'But why?' he asked. 'The kicks?'

'Partly, I suppose. But, I'm afraid, it's really the politics. As a nation we've become a teeny bit decadent, haven't we?'

'I'm not going to argue politics up here.' Boysie was threshing about in his mind. What could he do? It was utter checkmate. Iris was still chattering:

'I'm sorry you had to be so deeply involved, darling. It wasn't all an act in Menton – the bed bits, I mean. Originally, we had several plans; then the Duke's visit came up and, as I had you on a bit of string, we thought it was too good to miss. What happened to the Duke, by the way?'

'He's all right. Mostyn caught on.'

'Pity. How?'

'Had someone watching me in France. The kidnapping really did it, I think. You boobed there.'

'Oh no. My dear, that was really all a ghastly mistake. But you saw what happened to the culprit...'

'You did that?' Boysie twitched, remembering the naked corpse.

'No, that was Constantine – Quadrant to you. But I was present. It was all rather

251

nasty. Still, the man was a dolt.' She looked grave. 'Constantine? Is he...?'

''Fraid so.'

Iris nodded: 'That's the way it goes. Peter bought it as well: when we tackled the ground crew.' Once more she adjusted the throttles, and flicked down on a switch into the left arm of the control column yoke.

'There we are. On course at 40,000 feet. The auto-pilot can do the work for a while.'

The absurdity of the whole thing was making Boysie question his sanity. Here they were, chatting as calmly as a pair of lovers on a beach.

'Give me a cigarette, Boysie.'

'You don't like mine. Anyway, Iris, I'm going to give you one more chance. Turn this aeroplane around.' Deep inside, he meant it: whatever the consequences, or agony of fear.

'Oh, knickers! Don't be so silly; you can't do anything. Pass me my coat, there's a love.'

They had become so relaxed that he almost fell for it. He put out his left hand to pick the coat from the back of her seat. Iris's foot came up hard, smashing his right hand against the instrument panel. The revolver clattered down. But Iris was off balance. Boysie swung to the right, his left palm extended, fingers together, thumb pushed back to make a hard striking edge to his hand.

The blow caught Iris below, and behind, her right ear. Her face flashed with pain, then relaxed as she toppled across the seat arm. Boysie stood up and lifted her into the seat. She was going to be out for a long time. He only hoped that he had not done any permanent damage. Sliding his hands under her arms, he lifted her into the co-pilot's seat, fastened the safety straps, picked up the revolver and climbed into the pilot's position.

Boysie looked around. He could hear the jets quietly humming. Below, an endless cloudscape passed gently by; above there was bright sky stretching to infinity. The terror washed over him again. At 40,000 feet here he was, on his own among the mind-scrambling mass of controls and instruments. Beside the seat arm, there was a headset and throat microphone, plugged into a junction box on the left side of the cabin. He picked them up, snapped the microphone round his neck and adjusted the earphones. Static crackled like fire in his ears, and he remembered the little black box. Reaching out Boysie tugged it from the windscreen, dropped it to the floor and hit it down hard with the revolver butt. The static cleared, and, from a long way off, he heard a voice:

'One Four Five Echo. Do you read me?...

One Four Five Echo... Do you read me?...'

On the right arm of the control column yoke there was a red button marked with a white R/T. Boysie put out his hand, touching the yoke as though it might burn him. Experimentally, he pressed:

'Help!' said Boysie weakly, and feeling rather silly. 'Help!' He released the button.

'One Four Five Echo. We read you. You are on the plot now. Inform who is in command.'

Boysie once more depressed the button:

'Oakes, Special Security. I'm alone. Pilot unconscious. Get me down, for crying out loud.' He reflected that his plea sounded like that of a small boy stuck up a gum tree.

'Listen out, One Four Five Echo. We have you on special frequency. I will pass you to a pilot experienced with your aircraft.' Back in the control tower at Gayborough all thought of normal procedure had gone. Boysie found himself shivering. His body seemed to have turned against him – violent cramps of fright binding his arms and legs. Another voice came into the earphones, still weak:

'Oakes? I am going to assist you in landing this aircraft. Have you had any experience as a pilot?'

'No...'

'Do you know anything at all about flying?'

'Hardly. I don't like it!' It was a relief to admit fear.

'All right. We're all a bit scared from time to time. But the Vulture is very simple. It'll be as easy as falling off a log.'

The sentence was badly phrased. Boysie thought he was going to have diarrhoea.

'Tell me what you do know.' The controller might have been a lecturer, safe in a classroom. Boysie, like many who have an inherent fear of flying, took a morbid interest in articles on air safety and novels about commercial airlines. The bulk of his knowledge came from the pages of books like *The High and the Mighty*, or *Cone of Silence*.

'I know that if I push the column forward the nose will go down, and vice versa. That the rudder pedals will turn the thing to the left and right; and that moving the yoke from side to side will give you bank to left and right.'

'Good. Before we do anything else you have got to turn the aircraft off its present course. We have you on a radar plot here and I am going to guide you. There is a switch on the left arm of the yoke. Is it down?'

'Yes. She said something about the auto-pilot.'

'She?'

'Woman pilot.'

'All right. You are being flown by the auto-pilot. Before you try your first turn, that switch will have to be in the off position – I will tell you when. Make yourself comfortable at the controls and fasten the safety harness. Feet on the rudder pedals; hands on the control yoke. Right?'

Gingerly Boysie settled himself:

'OK.'

'Now listen carefully. In the centre of the panel in front of you, there are six instruments, in two banks of three. The middle one in the top line is your artificial horizon. During the turn try to keep the centre of the white needle steady on the white line. You will find that the needle will give you the aircraft's altitude in reference to the horizon, so watch it. Do not try too much bank, just slew the plane round on the rudder. Do not make any sudden movements with the controls unless absolutely necessary. Have you got that?'

'I think so.'

'Good. Very soon now, I am going to count down from five to zero. At zero I want you to switch off the auto-pilot and depress the right – repeat right – rudder pedal. Watch your artificial horizon and do not let the nose drop. Give a little gentle bank to the right and keep the aircraft turning to the right until I tell you to level off. Do you understand?'

Boysie could feel the blood pumping in his head:

'Yes. I'll try it.'

'I am following your course on the plot here. You have noting to worry about. Ready?'

'Ready.'

'Here we go then. Coming up now. Five... Four... Three... Two... One... Zero...'

Boysie flicked off the auto-pilot and carefully pressed forward with his right foot, moving the yoke slightly to the right. The needle on the artificial horizon tilted, but he seemed to remain steady. From the corner of his eye, he could see the compass – forward of the control pedestal and throttles – swing round.

It was comparatively easy. Boysie even found himself enjoying the sense of power over the machine. When the turn was completed, the controller instructed him to switch back on to the auto-pilot. Boysie glanced across at Iris, still sleeping peacefully.

The controller was on again:

'You will soon have to begin your descent. You are on course for Gayborough and we plan to guide you straight on to the runway. I want you to switch off the auto-pilot again and try the controls: get the feel of them; very gently: give you confidence. Don't lift or drop the nose too high or low. All right. Go ahead, I'm watching you on the plot. If you are worried, yell out: nothing can go very wrong at your present height.'

Once more Boysie switched off the auto-pilot. The aircraft responded sharply to every touch. He could feel the nose swing and the cabin tilt. The sensation was exhilarating: the power of command. For the first time in his life – under what should have been the most terrifying circumstances – Boysie was enjoying the flight. He straightened the aircraft and again put on the auto-pilot.

'All right?' said the controller.

'Fine.'

'Now I want you to locate certain essential instruments before you begin to let down. We have about five minutes. You know where the throttles are?'

'Yes.'

'Behind them you will see a similar lever marked in black. Got it?'

'Yes.'

'Flaps control. You can see that it is graded fractionally.'

'Yes.'

'OK, Oakes, you are doing fine. To the right there is a similar lever; with a red knob. Got that one?'

'Yes.'

'Dive brakes. Now, to the rear of the control pedestal there is a curved handle.'

'I can see that: marked "Undercarriage.

Up and Down".'

'Undercarriage. Yes, good. In front of you, on the right of the instrument panel there is a white switch marked "P".'

'Yes, I can see it.'

'Braking parachute. I'll tell you when to use that – just after your wheels touch the ground.' The voice was quite clear now. 'You operate the main wheel brakes by pushing down on the rudder pedals – very gently. I am not going to bother you with anything else. We have no time. Use your common sense and do exactly as I say. The idea is to bring you right down on to the runway. Your main job will be to keep the aircraft level and in line with the runway. Try to get her down as near to the boundary as possible. Is that clear?'

'As it ever will be. I'd rather get cracking.'

'OK. We will begin the descent. Take out the auto-pilot. Hold her straight and level, wait for my instructions. Repeat orders to me when you have performed them. Clear?'

'Clear.'

'When I tell you to put the nose down, watch the artificial horizon and hold the aircraft so that the needle is just below the white line. I want you on a gentle dive. Stand by.'

Boysie switched out the auto-pilot and waited: incredibly calm. He wondered if this was the same kind of coolness that was supposed to come to men under sentence of death.

'You ready?'

'Yes. Auto-pilot out.'

'Here we go then. Throttles back.'

'Throttles back.'

'Dive brakes out.'

'Dive brakes out.'

'Gently, down with the nose.'

'Nose down.'

Boysie felt the engine power fade.

'Nose is dropping too far. I can't hold her.'

'Ease back on the column. Hold her. All right.'

'Got her now.'

The aircraft was more difficult to handle and there seemed to be a hissing noise outside the cabin. He was in a shallow dive, heading straight for the massive sea of cloud below.

'Can you see your altimeter?'

'Damn thing whizzing round like a clock gone mad?'

'That'll be it. You should be losing about 6,000 a minute.'

Minutes seemed like hours. He was in cloud now: wedged in on all sides by a thick white floss. The machine was bumping; swaying; difficult to hold steady. The sweat was returning, running down his face, salty at the corners of his mouth; and he could feel the singing whine in his ears.

'Watch your speed. Sorry, I mean lift the nose slightly: you're coming down a shade too fast.'

The aircraft broke through the cloud. Boysie's stomach jumped. The ground was spread out on a great patterned carpet below him. He seemed suspended, angled above it.

'Nose up a fraction.'

'Am I all right?'

'You're doing fine.'

The pattern below him was clearer.

'The field's over to your right. Swing to your right. Right rudder. That's enough. Now level out.'

Boysie had an uncanny feeling that he was hanging, immobile in the sky. Then he realised the features on the ground were much larger.

'Open your throttles about a quarter.'

'Right.'

The aircraft surged forward.

'Dive brakes in.'

'Dive brakes in.'

'Look down at the pedestal and push the flaps' lever to one-third.'

'Flaps one-third.'

'Undercarriage down. Keep her level.'

'Undercarriage down.' Three green lights winked up at Boysie from the instrument panel.

'Your wheels are down. We can see you. You

are too far to the right. Left rudder. More. Can you see the runway? Dead ahead.'

Boysie could see what looked like a tiny oblong of grey and black ribbon. Suddenly it was picked out by two rows of yellow dots.

'We have put the runway lights on for you. Two-thirds flap.'

'Two-thirds flap.'

He was nose down and losing height rapidly: the runway, looking very small, but getting nearer and nearer.

'Full flap.'

'Full flap.'

'Throttles right back.'

'Throttles back.'

'Don't let her nose go up. You're swinging right. Left rudder. Hold her level... Just keep her level ... level...'

A road came up and flashed past, away to his right. He thought he could see children waving in a field. They seemed to be terribly close. Everything was happening fast. Oak trees: bloody great oak trees. He was going to hit them. No. Well over the top. Now the edge of the airfield, straight ahead. The runway was racing up to meet him. He was going to smash straight into the ground. None of his muscles seemed to be co-operating.'

'Nose up a little. Fine. You're all right. Nose up ... up...'

He was practically on to the ground now.

The left wing seemed to be dropping. He corrected. The controls seemed sloppy. Now the nose was going down. The whole machine juddered as his right wheel touched. Then a bump on the left side.

'Column forward. Parachute! Parachute now!'

Boysie banged down on the switch. He was rocketing along the runway, the fence at the far end leaping towards him.

'Brake ... gently ... gently.'

The Vulture shuddered, screeched and slowly rolled to a standstill: the nose four feet from the grass which marked the end of the runway. Boysie's arms fell limply from the control column; the windscreen misted over and he passed out.

They had to break down the door to get on to the flight deck. Boysie was still sitting at the controls, dazed, near-paralysed with shock. Iris came-to as the service policemen lifted her out of the aircraft. She bit one of them, painfully, on the ear; and ruptured the other with her beautiful knee.

There were four men in the station sick bay. Flavell, the Vulture's pilot, two of his crew and one member of his ground crew: all injured during the fight, when Iris and her group had suddenly appeared – in disguise – at the dispersal point.

In the little mortuary, next to the sick bay,

there were four bodies. Two of the Vulture's ground crew; the big, bald Peter; and a corpse with large protruding ears who had, in life, been Constantine Alexei Skabichev.

'Well, old Oakes, we're obviously not in a position to use you in your former dramatic role, are we?' It was early evening. Mostyn, his arm white-slinged and interesting, sat facing Boysie in the sick bay. The Duke had just gone, and Boysie felt incredibly pleased with himself. True, his legs still seemed to be made of slightly tacky blancmange, and his guts continued to perform odd circular motions. But the Duke had been most complimentary.

The most pleasant thought, however, was that he could now sneak out of the Department with no one any the wiser about his duplicity. Mostyn's remark had clinched it. He grinned:

'Afraid this is where we part company,' he said smugly.

'Oh, I don't think it need come to that,' said Mostyn. 'I've got lots of ideas. We can always use a man like you. Don't usually pass out the compliments, old Boysie, but you did a very brave thing this morning. The RAF boys are thrilled to bits.'

Oh God, thought Boysie. If only Mostyn knew. He never wanted to hear of the Department again: he never wanted to see another aeroplane, let alone fly in one. Death would come soon enough without tempting it closer.

'Well, honestly, sir,' he started. 'I think it would be better if I left the Service. I'd be happier...'

'But we'd be sad, old Boysie. Nonsense, we can't think of letting you go. If it hadn't been for you...'

Boysie knew he had lost.

'Take a month's leave and then we'll talk about it. I'm going to have most of my time cut out interrogating that blasted Iris. She sent you a message, by the way – before they took her to London. Shouldn't worry, though, it's physically impossible – unless you're a hermaphrodite.'

There was a tap at the door. The doctor ushered Black Angus into the room.

'The Station Commander wants to know if you two feel well enough to come over to the Mess for a while,' said the doctor.

'I think a wee dram would be in order.' Black Angus was beaming.

'OK by me,' said the doctor.

The party was in full swing. At the far end of the bar, Mostyn was deep in slurred conversation with Martin – now sporting a large cigar – and the Group Captain. All around there was the slop and slush of a high old time in the Mess.

Boysie regarded the tall WRAF officer's knees with immense respect. They were knees in a thousand: jewels between perfect calves and, what appeared to be, most satisfying thighs. She looked at him, adoringly, with the smoky-grey eyes he had first seen across the busy control tower earlier in the day.

'You couldn't possibly slip away from here for a week or two, could you?' said Boysie.

'Well, as a matter of fact, I have got some leave due,' said the WRAF officer, whose name was Inez.

'Well then: how about a spot of holiday? Just the two of us? I'm on leave for a month.'

'Where can we go?'

'You choose.'

'I adore the South of France,' said Inez. 'I'll have a word with the Adjutant, but I'm sure it'll be all right. I knew, Boysie, the moment I saw you, I knew: about us. Perhaps we could fly to Nice or somewhere. We might even get away tonight. London, and then the Côte D'Azur.'

'Yes,' said Boysie, gulping his pink gin and turning his head to hide the twitch that was developing down the left side of his face. 'Yes, that would be lovely.'

But Inez did not hear. She was up and across the room, talking to the Adjutant. Some of the conversation floated back:

'Honestly, Adj., it's very urgent... I must get off tonight... Yes... Oh jolly good.'

Hooked, thought Boysie. Bloody hooked again.

The publishers hope that this book has given you enjoyable reading. Large Print Books are especially designed to be as easy to see and hold as possible. If you wish a complete list of our books please ask at your local library or write directly to:

Magna Large Print Books
Magna House, Long Preston,
Skipton, North Yorkshire.
BD23 4ND

This Large Print Book, for people
who cannot read normal print,
is published under the auspices of

THE ULVERSCROFT FOUNDATION